RHINO FIRE

Elizabeth Laird was born in New Zealand but when she was two the family moved to England. Since then she has travelled to the furthest corners of the world and has encountered all kinds of animals. On one adventure she became lost at night in a Kenyan game reserve, coming a little too close to an angry rhino and narrowly avoiding buffalo and elephants. Her experience of the wild animals of Africa has helped her write the *Wild Things* series.

She is the award-winning author of *Red Sky in the Morning*, *Kiss the Dust*, *Secret Friends* (shortlisted for the 1997 Carnegie Medal) and many other children's novels.

Elizabeth Laird has been helped in her research for *Wild Things* by wildlife experts and local people in Kenya, whose lives are constantly touched by the animals amongst which they live.

D1041247

Books available in the Wild Things series

1. Leopard Trail
2. Baboon Rock
3. Elephant Thunder
4. Rhino Fire

Coming soon

5. Red Wolf   October 1999

All Wild Things titles can be ordered at your local bookshop or are available by post from Book Service by Post (tel: 01624 675137).

WILD THINGS

RHINO FIRE

Elizabeth Laird

MACMILLAN CHILDREN'S BOOKS

*Series consultant: Dr Shirley Strum
with the support of Dr David Western,
past director of the Kenya Wildlife Service*

First published 1999 by Macmillan Children's Books
a division of Macmillan Publishers Limited
25 Eccleston Place, London SW1W 9NF
Basingstoke and Oxford
www.macmillan.co.uk

Associated companies throughout the world

ISBN 0 330 37151 7

Copyright © Elizabeth Laird 1999

The right of Elizabeth Laird to be identified as the
author of this work has been asserted by her in accordance
with the Copyright, Designs and Patents Act 1988.

All rights reserved. No part of this publication may be
reproduced, stored in or introduced into a retrieval system,
or transmitted, in any form, or by any means (electronic, mechanical,
photocopying, recording or otherwise) without the prior written
permission of the publisher. Any person who does any unauthorized
act in relation to this publication may be liable to criminal
prosecution and civil claims for damages.

1 3 5 7 9 8 6 4 2

A CIP catalogue record for this book is available from
the British Library.

Phototypeset by Intype London Ltd
Printed and bound in Great Britain by Mackays of Chatham plc, Kent

This book is sold subject to the condition that it shall not,
by way of trade or otherwise, be lent, re-sold, hired out,
or otherwise circulated without the publisher's prior consent
in any form of binding or cover other than that in which
it is published and without a similar condition including this
condition being imposed on the subsequent purchaser.

For Densu Moseti and Saumu Bibo

because their father, Tim Oloo, who is a rhino expert, showed me the rare black rhinos in Nakuru National Park. He's been chased many times by rhinos, but he's still alive to tell the tale.

The freshness of morning still cooled the air, though the vaporous mist had already burnt off the vast landscape. A slight breeze rattled the leaves of the sparse acacia trees and rustled in the clumps of bushes growing beneath them.

Other sounds, too, carried across the sweeping hillsides, the chattering of a flock of starlings, the occasional bark of a baboon and, far away, the rumble of traffic as trucks changed gear on the busy main road.

The rhino had fed well during the night and had been walking his range since before dawn. He took the same route every day, visiting his favourite bushes, pulling the tips of shoots into his mouth with his mobile upper lip, then biting them off with his teeth. Carefully he marked his trail as he went, leaving his scent for any other rhino to pick up, and diligently he too sniffed for any sign that another of his species had wandered across his path.

He found nothing. All was as it had been for many seasons now. He was alone.

He came to the thick stand of bushes where he

always passed the hottest part of the day and took up his usual position, standing in the deep shade, one forefoot tilted forward, his head with its two great horns lowered, resting. Even the oxpecker, the busy red-billed bird who lived on his back, feeding on his ticks, was still.

On the road down in the valley below, a truck backfired twice, and the noise rang out like the sound of shots. The rhino lifted his head and jerked it up and down angrily, as if horning a phantom enemy. He had heard sounds like that long ago, once even very close at hand. He had been little more than a calf then, newly weaned and separated from his mother, and he had come upon her body, covered in blood, lying still on the ground. Beside it was her new calf, his sister, mewing piteously. He had circled round them for a while, gently butting his dead mother with his nose, peering through his myopic eyes at the strange stumps on her head where her horns had been savagely sawn off.

Then he had moved helplessly away. The calf had tried to follow him but he had had no milk for her. She had copied him, nibbling at the plants he ate, but two days later she too had fallen down and lain still.

The truck with the faulty exhaust had nearly reached the top of the hill now, and as it changed gear it backfired again. The rhino skittered with fright and retreated further back into the haven *of bushes. He would stay there as he always did until the sun was past its height, then he would resume his solitary round, the sole survivor of his prehistoric race in this vast landscape.*

1

HELICOPTER CHASE

Joseph looked nervously out of the helicopter. He'd never flown in one before. The machine was high above the tops of the acacia trees, and the ground was a very long way down. He could see the shadow of the helicopter racing over the land below like a grey spirit. It was scary.

He was just trying to estimate his chances of survival if the thing crashed, when Afra, the girl in the seat beside him, grabbed his arm. Joseph turned to look at her.

'Elephants! Look!' she shouted above the deafening roar of the engine.

He leaned across her to peer out of the window on her side of the helicopter. Below, a herd of elephants was racing over the dusty ground. Their huge grey backs were dwarfed from this height but he was amazed to see how fast they could run, their great grey legs loping gracefully over the brown earth between the trees, their trunks swinging in front of them.

The helicopter swerved suddenly.

'There!' shouted the pilot. 'Near those rocks.'

The man beside him leaned out of the open

side of the helicopter, making Joseph catch his breath.

'Please, take care, Uncle Titus,' he yelled. 'Don't fall out!'

His uncle ignored him. He was speaking now into the microphone attached to his radio headset.

'Listen, Omondi, we've found the male rhino,' he said. 'Repeat: found male rhino. We are closing in for darting. Do you read me, over?'

Afra nudged Joseph again.

'I can't hear. What's he saying?'

Joseph, his fear forgotten, was eagerly leaning forward, looking straight ahead between his uncle and the pilot through the glass nose of the helicopter.

'There!' he shouted. 'A rhino! He's a fast one.'

Afra was leaning forward too now.

'I don't see the truck,' she yelled. 'Where's the ground team?'

Titus Musau looked round and frowned at them. 'Be quiet, you kids. I can't hear the radio.'

He was easing himself ever further out of the helicopter, the long dart gun in his hands. He lifted it to his shoulder and took aim.

Joseph glanced sideways at Afra. Her eyes were tight shut and her fists were clenched. He knew what she was thinking. She was hating the idea of the drugged dart plunging into the rhino's unsuspecting flesh, of the powerful, noble creature crashing to his knees. She was hating the thought that he might be frightened or hurt or humiliated.

But they've got to do it, he thought, silently arguing with her. It's the only way the rhinos can be saved.

Titus fired, and Joseph saw the rhino spurt forward. They were still too far away to see the gleam of the silver dart sticking into his dun coloured rump, but Joseph knew it would be there.

Uncle Titus is the best shot in Kenya, he thought proudly.

Titus was speaking into the microphone again, calling up Omondi, the rhino expert, and his ground team in the truck.

'He's hit,' Joseph heard him shout. He looked back and down and saw the heavy green truck with its enormous wooden crate bouncing along the rough ground, coming in at right-angles towards the path of the helicopter.

'Go left.' Titus was instructing the truck driver through the radio. 'About a hundred and fifty metres. He's still running. Going straight. Can you see him yet?'

Joseph could hear the faint crackle of the answer coming through Titus's earphones.

'Affirmative,' Titus said. 'He's slowing down. Go forward. Now right a bit. Yes! You're behind him. Stay where you are. We're coming down. Over.'

The pilot banked suddenly and Joseph's

stomach rose and fell, driving the breath half out of him. Then the helicopter was hovering a few metres above a bare patch of earth, raising a storm of dust as it slowly dropped down to meet the ground.

Titus had tumbled out before it had landed and was sprinting through the sparse acacia trees towards the gleaming bulk of the truck. Afra and Joseph scrambled down after him, ducking under the still flailing blades of the helicopter. They raced after him, their feet crunching on the dry herbs and shrubs that covered the bare ground.

The rhino was still running, his huge angry body crashing through the dry bushes, but he was staggering, lurching from side to side as if he was drunk.

There were a dozen people or more on his trail now. Titus, Joseph and Afra from the helicopter were running behind John Omondi, the rhino expert, and his nine trackers from the truck. Behind them came Dr Ibrahim, the stout vet, who panted along at the rear, encumbered by his heavy equipment case.

Ahead, Joseph could see that the rhino had slowed to a walking pace and the pursuers had slowed too, Titus in front, his hand held up for silence. Everyone was quiet, waiting for the drug to take hold and the rhino to sink to the ground, wanting him to keep calm so that he didn't panic and struggle against the anaesthetic.

To his horror, Joseph felt a sneeze gathering momentum in his nose. He wrinkled his nostrils, pinched at the bridge of his nose with his fingers and rubbed at it frantically, but the sneeze was too strong for him. It burst out like a pistol shot, making everyone jump.

The rhino had been still for a moment, his great head, weighed down by its heavy cargo of horn, drooping towards the ground, but a judder went through him at the sound and he began to run again, swaying dangerously into a narrow ravine where giant boulders had crashed down the hillside making it almost impassable.

'Joseph!' Titus's voice was like a whiplash. 'I knew you were stupid. I didn't know you were disobedient too.'

Afra's eyebrows flew up. She'd never heard Titus speak to his favourite nephew like that before.

'He couldn't help it!' she began indignantly, but Titus had turned on his heel and was following the rhino into the ravine.

Afra turned to Joseph.

'Phew! What was that about?'

'He's angry with me,' Joseph whispered miserably, hanging back while the ground team went ahead. 'Mama told him about my bad results in science. He shouted at me so much I thought he would beat me like my dad used to.'

'Titus? He'd never lay a finger on you.' Afra

shook her mop of dark curly hair decisively. 'He adores you. You know that. Look, the rhino's down. Come on, let's go see.'

'You go. I don't care.'

'You don't *what*? There's an unconscious rhino out here in the wild, you're helping to save him from certain death by poachers, and you don't *care*?'

'Leave me alone, Afra. You don't have to attack me too.'

Joseph, who was tall for his thirteen years, glared down at her.

Afra flashed him a quick grin.

'OK, I'm sorry. Let's leave this for later. Come on!'

She pulled at Joseph's sleeve and began to run on light feet after the men. Joseph shook her off, and followed more slowly.

Dr Ibrahim, the vet, was already kneeling awkwardly on the ground beside the huge fallen body, his case of drugs and equipment open. He was filling a syringe, holding it up to check that it was full.

He got to his feet and brushed the red dust off the knees of his khaki bush trousers.

'We'll have to walk him out,' he said. 'Titus, put the blindfold on him before I give him a shot to get him back on his feet.'

Joseph, not wanting to get in the way, walked cautiously round the outside of the group of men who were working around the fallen rhino, and came up near the great creature's head. He had crashed over onto his side. His short legs, encased in a wrinkled leathery hide, looked oddly vulnerable. His massive head lay motionless, the pair of powerful horns, the longest one on the tip of his nose, the shorter one behind it, lying defenceless in the dust.

'Oh, that's so awful. Look, his eyes are open.' Afra had followed Joseph and was looking down at the rhino with horror and compassion. 'He's so grand and noble and now he looks kind of . . . I don't know . . . humiliated.'

The rhino's small black eye stared unseeingly from its bloodshot rim. He scarcely blinked as the uniformed rangers, working with frantic speed, laid a blindfold over his head then began to tie ropes round his legs and body.

One rope caught on the rhino's left ear and a ranger tugged it free. Afra winced, gave a little cry and put out a hand as if to give the ear a comforting stroke. Joseph dragged her away.

'Don't be foolish. You'll slow them down.'

'They don't have to be so rough,' Afra said indignantly. 'They could take a little time to be gentle.'

John Omondi was nearest her. He was sweating with the effort of lifting one of the great feet to slip a rope round it, but he looked over his shoulder at her and grunted.

'There is no time. Every moment he is under the anaesthetic it is dangerous for him. Do you want him to die?'

Joseph and Afra retreated from the rhino's head towards his rump, where Titus and Dr Ibrahim were working.

Titus had pulled the dart out of the rhino's thick hide and had laid it down on a stone. Joseph saw it as he approached and, wanting to be helpful, picked it up.

'Where do you want to put this, Uncle Titus?' he said.

Titus glanced up from the notes he was making.

'Put that down at once!' He spoke so sharply that several of the rangers turned round to look. 'For heaven's sake, boy, that stuff knocks out a rhino. You prick your finger on it and you'll be out cold in one minute. Give it to me.'

With infinite caution, Joseph handed the dart to Titus.

'Put it in my kit,' growled Dr Ibrahim. 'I told you, Titus, you shouldn't have put it down there.'

He turned back to the rhino, a syringe in his hand.

'Ready?' he called out to Omondi, at the rhino's head. 'I'm giving him the shot now. Partial resuscitation. Get the ropes braced.'

Titus shot a furious look at Joseph.

'Keep out of the way, both of you. I'm crazy. I should never have let you come.'

He went up to the head of the rhino and took his place on the rope beside Omondi. Dr Ibrahim pushed the needle into the rhino's thigh and the plunger went home. A shudder ran through the huge animal. Joseph's heart missed a beat. What if Dr Ibrahim had given him too much of the restorative drug? What if the rhino really came to, and went berserk? He wanted to back away, but pride made him stand his ground. So what if everyone thought he was stupid? He wouldn't let them call him, a man of the Kamba tribe, a coward too.

The rhino's head had come up now, and he was lumbering to his feet. He was an enormous beast, a dense mass of muscle and hide and bone. He stood still, weaving his head from side to side, dazed by the drugs and disorientated by the blindfold.

Omondi gave the rangers a command and they began to pull on the ropes. The rhino took a few lurching steps and seemed about to fall to the ground again, but with an obvious effort of will he righted himself. The men were turning him now, speaking softly, pushing and tugging. The rhino broke in to a staggering trot and the men had to run to keep up with him.

'Left, go left now,' Omondi panted, looking through the trees for signs of the truck. 'That's right. Mwangi, tighten that rope. Bowa, come up to the head. Steer him round or we'll hit that tree.'

Joseph and Afra followed behind. Joseph, humiliated and smarting from his uncle's anger, was keeping well out of Titus's way. He looked sideways at Afra, hoping she would say something sympathetic, but she was watching the rhino as it slowed down to a groggy walk.

'It's just so wrong,' she burst out, 'putting animals through all this, risking their lives even.'

Joseph felt irritated.

'What do you want us to do, then?' he demanded. 'Leave them here, where there's no protection, so poachers can come in and kill them all off?'

'No, of course I don't. Don't be dumb, Joseph.'

He flinched. She looked at him in surprise.

'What's the problem?'

'*I am not dumb.* Just because I failed my science exam, everyone seems to think—'

'What?' Afra laughed. 'Oh boy, you really do care about that old exam, don't you? You know I don't think you're dumb, dumbo! Oops!'

Joseph didn't even smile.

'It's not just an old exam. It's the decider. It means they won't allow me to go on and try for the scholarship.'

'I thought Sarah was going to ask them if you could resit the exam.'

Joseph snorted.

'Mama can ask them, but what good will it do? Even if I take it again I'll fail. Chemistry! I hate it!' He put up his balled fists and boxed the air, as if fighting the hated subject away. 'It's all nonsense. It has nothing to do with anything.'

The rangers in front of them had almost reached the truck. Two of them raced ahead and lowered the ramp. The others braced themselves, ready to heave and push the heavy rhino up the ramp and into the crate.

Omondi broke into a Swahili chant.

'Come, fierce warrior, heave!
Come, my champion, heave!'

'Uh! Uh!' chanted the men in reply, putting their combined weight against the rhino's massive flanks.

The rhino stood his ground.

'Come, my wild one, heave!
Come, my brave one, heave!' chanted Omondi.

'Oh, oh!' answered the men, as they pushed again.

Joseph ran forward and laid his slim shoulder against the rhino's mighty buttock. It smelled pungent, a cow kind of smell, and he could feel the muscles quiver and contract as the rhino suddenly gave in and ran up the ramp into the crate.

The men gave a cry of triumph and slapped each other's hands. Dr Ibrahim turned to Titus.

'Excellent,' he said. 'Are you coming with us in the truck? Or do you want to return to Nairobi with the helicopter?'

Titus looked at his watch.

'I'll go back with the kids in the helicopter,' he said. 'We were going to visit my father on the way home, but now we don't have the time.' He turned to Afra and Joseph. 'Come on. Let's go.'

He began to walk towards the helicopter.

Joseph didn't move. An angry tide was welling up inside him.

'We're not going to visit Grandfather after all?' he demanded.

'No,' said Titus curtly. 'This has taken too long. We don't have the time.'

'He's expecting us,' said Joseph. 'He'll be disappointed.'

'I have already informed you,' said Titus, his handsome face stern with disapproval, 'that we do not have the time.'

Joseph felt his chest tightening. He summoned up his courage.

'Go without me, please, Uncle Titus,' he said stiffly. 'I'll go with the truck. They can leave me at the road junction and I'll walk to the village. It's only ten kilometres.'

'Hey, Joseph! Are you crazy?' cried Afra.

Titus's eyes opened in surprise and he looked intently at Joseph.

'You don't want to come to Nakuru with us?

You don't want to see this fellow' – he jerked his chin towards the crate on the truck – 'arrive in his new home?'

'I'll take the bus tomorrow,' said Joseph, with all the dignity he could muster. 'I'll come to Nakuru after I've visited my grandfather.'

A gleam of understanding and amusement shone for a moment in Titus's eyes, then he turned back to the helicopter.

'As you like. We'll see you tomorrow. Greet my father for me, Joseph. Tell him his grandson is like him, as stubborn as a rhino!'

2

GRANDFATHER'S VILLAGE

Joseph set off up the track away from the main road where the truck had dropped him off. It had rained recently and the thick mud soon caked his shoes but he was too preoccupied to notice. He was furious with everyone: with his stupid science teacher who had got him so confused and then failed him in the crucial test; with Sarah, his mother, who had burst into tears and told him if he wanted to end up a no-hoper like his father he was going the right way about it; with Afra, who was supposed to be his friend, practically his sister, since they'd grown up together, but who cared more about a rhino, or any animal for that matter, than she cared about him; and most of all, with Uncle Titus, the man more than any other in the whole world that he looked up to, and whose good opinion he would do anything for. He'd known Titus would be disappointed if he failed to get the scholarship that would give him a chance in a decent school at last, but he hadn't expected his uncle's anger to erupt so fiercely. He hadn't expected contempt.

He walked fast. It was a long way, a good

two hours' walk, to his grandfather's village. The stream that ran down the valley floor beside the track was swollen by the recent rain. It was cutting new channels through the soft red African earth, carrying away in its turbulent eddies whole slices of crumbling banks.

Uncle Titus ought to have come, he thought self-righteously. We promised. Grandfather's expecting us.

He knew, though, that duty to his grandfather wasn't the only reason he'd wanted to come. It wasn't even the real reason. Grandfather was the only person who wouldn't be angry with him. Grandfather had never taken an exam in his life. He knew there were other things that mattered, other things a man could do. Joseph always felt good when he was with Grandfather, as if the bits of himself that had been separated were coming together. It was a solid, comfortable feeling. A family feeling.

The stream had obviously flooded recently and the old wooden bridge had been washed away. Someone had laid logs across it to make a rough and ready replacement. Joseph was too preoccupied to notice. He stepped onto the new bridge and felt one of the logs rock beneath his feet. The movement jarred him out of his thoughts and he looked up, suddenly aware of his surroundings.

He'd had cousins living near here when he was younger, and they'd often played with him down by the stream. They'd picked maize cobs and tomatoes out of the water that the floods had washed down from the fields above. They'd played games of Jacks with little stones and modelled things out of the sticky mud. He'd always loved it here. He and Mama hadn't come very often from Nairobi but whenever they had, it had felt like home.

I wish we all still lived around here, he thought, like Mama and Titus and all of them did when they were young.

Everyone was scattered now. His older sister, Monica, lived down on the coast. He hardly ever saw her. His cousins had moved away, following their parents into the outskirts of Nairobi. Titus and Mama both lived in Nairobi now.

And no one even knows where my father is, he thought bitterly.

It was funny, but he hadn't thought about his father for a long time. Father had been so stern and remote, so ready with his stick, so angry with the slightest fault, that Joseph had felt nothing but relief when he'd disappeared seven years ago to find work abroad. There had been a few postcards, first from Zimbabwe and then from Zambia, but no news had come for years now.

'He's supposed to be my father but he doesn't care if I'm alive or dead,' said Joseph out loud, and he broke into a trot as if to shake the uncomfortable thought away.

High hedges of prickly pear lined the path now, the flat fleshy leaves studded with vicious spines. He heard a noise from behind one of them, a dry rustling sound, and bent down to look through a gap into the field beyond.

A porcupine, disturbed from its resting place, had trotted out from behind the hedge, its black and white quills lying like thick coarse fur on its back. It stopped moving, nervously aware of Joseph's presence, took fright properly and with a violent rattling noise raised its quills and shook them, turning itself at once into a fortress of bristling prickles.

Joseph snorted with sudden laughter and the porcupine scuttled away in an ungainly gallop across the field.

'I know how you feel,' Joseph called out after him. 'Keep your quills up! You need them.'

Some buildings were in sight now. A few small shops and houses, roofed with corrugated iron and painted in bright colours, clustered at the head of the valley, where the track took a sharp turn and started climbing the steep hill.

Joseph went up to one of the small shops whose whole frontage formed a high counter.

'A kilo of sugar, please,' he said to the man in the shop.

The man weighed the sugar and handed the packet down to him.

'Joseph Mutua, isn't it?' he said in a surly voice.

'About time one of your family showed your face here. Your grandfather needs you all around him now. He's an old man. Your mama should take him to live in her house.'

Joseph said nothing but he felt his face darken as the blood rose in his cheeks. He took the sugar and went on, beginning the stiff climb up to his grandfather's house.

'He's insulting me and my mother,' he muttered angrily. 'I'm nearly a man! Why should he speak to me like that?'

His grandfather was sitting outside his house on a three-legged stool when Joseph arrived at last at the clump of trees that stood above the small house. He was leaning back against the patched and crumbling walls, shaded by the ragged thatch that spilled off the deep eaves overhead. His eyes were closed.

Joseph went up to the old man softly. He didn't want to startle him. He squatted down in front of him and coughed gently.

Old Kimeu woke up at once and saw Joseph in front of him.

'Eh, eh, my grandson. I am happy to see you. I've waited for this for many days.' He looked over Joseph's shoulder. 'Where's Titus?'

Joseph put his hand on his grandfather's knee.

'He couldn't come. He sent you his greeting.'

'What is this, he couldn't come, he couldn't come?'

Kimeu's face dropped again. His eyes, filmed with cataracts, clouded over.

'He's sorry, Grandfather,' said Joseph respectfully.

The old man reached down to the ground for his stick with his right hand and put his left on Joseph's shoulder, leaning on him as he got to his feet. He was wearing an old shirt and a pair of khaki cotton shorts and Joseph saw how the mahogany-coloured skin on his ancient knees hung loose, and how slowly his grandfather was straightening himself.

He really is old, he thought.

Kimeu waved his stick towards a big woman who was crossing the open ground beside a house just below.

'Eh, Mwende, bring something to drink. My grandson's here.'

Joseph waved to the women. She was Grandfather's niece. She looked after him now.

'I've brought you both a present,' he called to her. 'Some sugar.'

Mwende smiled and called something, but old Kimeu was already ducking his head under the low lintel of his house, and Joseph followed him inside, carrying his stool.

It was dark in the house. A little light came in through the door and cracks in the wall where the mud had crumbled away. Joseph needed time for his eyes to adjust.

A small fire was burning on the ground. Kimeu settled himself on his stool and stirred the burning wood to make the sparks fly up.

'How is my grandson?' he said. 'Tell me your news.'

'Oh Grandfather,' Joseph burst out. 'I failed my science exam and they're all angry with me, Mama and Uncle Titus and everyone. I don't know what to do.'

A rusty chuckle rose in Kimeu's throat.

'Exams,' he said. 'That's all they think about nowadays. Exams! When I was a boy exams were different. To look after the cattle well, that was our exam. To learn to hunt well, and to defend yourself with your spear, to suffer pain without a cry, to respect your elders, those were our exams.'

Joseph fed the fire with a couple of sticks and sat quietly on the mat, looking into the leaping flames. He was feeling better already.

'Have you obeyed your mother and your uncle?' Kimeu said, passing a calloused hand over his bald head, which was edged by a fan of white hair.

Joseph nodded.

'Have you run away from your enemies or displayed cowardice? Have you been disloyal to your friends?'

Joseph shook his head.

'Then you're a good boy. A good Kamba.'

Joseph wriggled his toes inside his shoes.

'I wish I'd been born in your days. I wish I didn't have to go to school.'

Kimeu laughed out loud this time.

'No, no, modern times are good. Look at you, how many things you can do, how many things you know, more than me, and I am your own grandfather. I've lived in this village all my life. Do you want to do that?'

'I wouldn't mind,' said Joseph. 'I like it here.'

For a moment they sat in a companionable silence watching the flames, which had died down now, lick lazily round a charred log. Outside, the sudden African night had fallen and it was nearly dark. Joseph could hear Mwende, who was growing stout, panting as she climbed the steep slope to Kimeu's house.

She came in through the door and Joseph stood up to be hugged.

'There,' she said, balancing the dish and the bottles she was carrying carefully in her hands as she put her arms awkwardly round him. 'You're with your grandfather. Now look, some sodas for you. And eggs.'

She uncovered the dish and showed Joseph some hard-boiled eggs, then stood smiling at him, one hand on her hip.

'How is your ma? And Titus?'

'Joseph will come to visit you later,' Kimeu said impatiently.

Mwende took the hint and bent down to go out through the low doorway again.

'Mind you do, now,' she said. 'I'll be waiting for you.'

Kimeu picked up an egg and began to peel it.

'Why did you fail your exam?' he said. 'Were you lazy? Did you not work?'

'Yes! I worked so hard!' Joseph thought briefly of the science book he'd hardly had the courage to open, that had slipped off the little table where he worked at home and probably still lay behind it. 'At least, well, I couldn't. I can't understand it, Grandfather. I kept asking the teacher so many questions. He's no good. He doesn't want to answer me. In the end he sent for Mama and complained I was a troublemaker. But I'm not! It's just that I can't understand it all! Especially chemistry. It doesn't mean anything. It's all a muddle.'

Kimeu said nothing.

'It's all these stupid codes, that are supposed to be what things are made of, and some of them join up to make new things and sort of change and do different things.'

Kimeu handed him a peeled egg. The moist solid white of it gleamed in the firelight.

'It sounds like people to me,' he said, cracking another egg. 'People join up together and make new things and change. Like families.'

'How would I know?' Joseph cried bitterly.

'Where's my family? I only ever see Mama, usually, and Titus comes sometimes, and Monica's never there. I hardly ever see you and I might as well not have a father at all.'

Kimeu looked up at him, and his old eyes, in spite of the cataracts, were sharp.

'Your father was a good man,' he said.

'Was?' said Joseph. 'But he's still alive.'

Kimeu threw a handful of eggshells into the fire, which crackled in response.

'Who knows?' he said. 'If he's alive, why didn't he come back?'

'Because he didn't like us,' said Joseph savagely. 'He was always angry. He shouted at Mama and he beat me all the time. Do you know what, Grandfather? I was happy when he left.'

Kimeu seemed not to hear him.

'Too ambitious. Disappointed in life,' he muttered, as if he was talking to himself. I told him many times, "Make the best of things. Do what you can. Be contented." But he had big ideas, that one. Jealous, always jealous of others. He wanted too much and he didn't see how many good things he already had.'

Joseph was sitting still, listening intently.

'Is that why he went? You mean he wanted something else?'

Kimeu smiled.

'He wanted everything. Money. Success. A car, even. The wrong things. He looked for happiness

26

in the wrong places. He drove himself. He was a good man, but a fool too. How can you tell, when you give your daughter to a man, how he will be?'

He was looking into the fire again, his hands, holding the half-peeled egg, motionless. He seemed to have forgotten Joseph.

Joseph coughed, and Kimeu looked up at him and smiled.

'Joseph, you're not like your father. You're a good boy. The best grandson. Titus is like a father to you now. Obey him. If he wants a scholarship for you, he's right. You must work harder. Try harder.'

Joseph hunched his shoulders uncomfortably.

'This village life is past,' Kimeu went on. 'Nothing is like it was. Look at you. When I was your age, I was circumcized. As the knife cut into my tenderest place I knew the most terrible pain. If I had cried out then my family would have been shamed. All of us, we had to bear it. And the preparations, the celebrations . . .'

Joseph had heard the story of his grandfather's circumcision many times before. He listened impatiently as the old man told it again.

'At least you didn't have exams,' he said at last, when the familiar story came to an end.

Kimeu laughed, and put a hand on Joseph's knee.

'Perhaps exams are your circumcision. For us,

27

to become men, we carried the pain in our bodies. You must carry it in your head. That's how you will become a man.'

Joseph said nothing. Kimeu gave his shoulder a little shake.

'Well then, I tell you what I'll do. Work hard, Joseph, take the exam again. If you pass it the next time, I'll give you what my father gave to me. I'll give you a goat.'

3

THE RHINO'S BOMA

Joseph walked up the tarmac track towards the big main gates of Nakuru National Park. The double fences, both inner and outer ones, that surrounded the whole park, stretched away on both sides into the distance. It had been a long day and he was very tired. He'd left his grandfather's house just after dawn, and had walked fast back to the road. There'd been a long wait there. The rackety little *matatu* buses had sped past him, crammed full of people, and it wasn't until ten o'clock that he'd found a seat on one. Then, at the bus station in Nairobi, he'd had the same problem all over again.

He was here at last, though. He could see the waving crests of the fever trees in the thick forest that edged the lake in the centre of the game park. In spite of his nervousness at the thought of seeing Uncle Titus, a shiver of excitement ran through him. Leopards lived in those trees, and even lions climbed them sometimes, while in the thick bushes underneath pythons lay coiled, waiting for their prey to stumble across them. The rhino, too, must have arrived by now. He'd be in his acclimatizing pen, his *boma*, still a bit confused, and angry too, maybe. Rhinos had been known to break out of their *bomas* sometimes, Joseph knew. He suddenly felt anxious for Afra and Uncle Titus.

He was at the gate now. There was a lodge at one side of it, manned by the rangers of the Kenya Wildlife Service, but it seemed to be empty. Then he saw that a group of rangers were sitting on chairs just beyond it, absorbed in their conversation. He rattled the gate, hoping to attract their attention. One of them looked up, but, clearly unimpressed by the slim young boy in his travel-stained clothes, he didn't bother to get up.

'What do you want?' he called out.

'I'm Titus Musau's nephew,' Joseph shouted back. 'He's expecting me.'

Usually he felt proud when he said those words, knowing the respect everyone felt for his uncle, but now he felt only wary. Titus would be angry with him for going off like that, walking away from the amazing treat of riding in the helicopter, a treat he and Afra had begged for for months.

The ranger had jumped up at once at the sound of Titus Musau's name and he was striding over to the gate, a key in his hand. He unlocked it and waved Joseph through.

'Mr Musau is over there,' he said, waving towards a cluster of grey stone buildings near the park gates.

Joseph walked slowly across the grass towards them. A ranger in a smart uniform was sitting on a chair on the veranda by the open door. He jumped up when he saw Joseph and went inside.

At once a man came out, crossing the grass towards Joseph with long strides. Joseph stood still. It was Uncle Titus.

'Joseph!' Titus Musau's voice was sharp and Joseph felt his stomach tighten. Then he realized that the sharpness was anxious rather than angry.

He smiled warily as Titus reached him and grasped his shoulders with both hands.

'Joseph! You are all right? You managed the journey all right?'

Joseph felt a surge of relief and pride.

'Yes, of course. I saw Grandfather. He's well. He sends you his greetings. I went to Nairobi on a *matatu* and came here by bus. How is he?'

'Who?' Titus looked puzzled.

'The rhino. Did he manage the journey all right? Is he used to his *boma* yet?'

Titus grinned.

'He's fine. A bit mad with us all, but he'll be OK. Anyway, never mind about the rhino. You're a rascal, young Joseph, you know that? I've been so worried about you.' He put his arm around Joseph's shoulders and they began to walk towards the building together. 'Afra's been giving me a hard time. She's terrible, that child. She has all the confidence of her American father and all

31

the strength of her African mother. Also she doesn't respect her elders.'

'Where is she?' said Joseph.

'Over there, in the rangers' quarters.' Titus waved a hand towards a wooded area beyond the nearest building. A troop of monkeys was chasing around noisily in the trees overhead. 'She keeps telling me I'm too hard on you. You couldn't help failing your exam because your teacher was no good.'

He stopped and turned to look down at Joseph. Joseph stood his gaze uncomfortably.

'He isn't any good, no,' he said. 'But it's not just him. It's science, especially chemistry. I hate it, Uncle Titus. I can't understand it. It's all so stupid and I get mixed up.'

A little frown appeared between Titus's strong eyebrows.

'Joseph, you must try again. You understand that, don't you? You've been so much with your friends, with Tom and Afra, I am afraid they've spoiled you. But Tom is British, and Afra's dad is American. They're rich, privileged kids. If they don't do well at school their fathers will look after them. They'll find a job somehow. But you – you must make your own way in the world. And if you don't get your scholarship—'

'I know, I know.' Joseph shook his head. He didn't want Uncle Titus to talk about it any more.

'I telephoned your school this morning,' Titus

said. 'They told me you can take the exam again, at the end of the holiday. They're going to give you another chance.'

Joseph felt an awful numbness creep through him.

I'll fail it again, he thought. I'll never understand all that science stuff.

Aloud he said, 'Thank you, Uncle Titus. I'll do my best.'

'Well, we won't talk about it again while we're here,' said Titus, trying to sound jovial. 'Have your break here. You deserve it, after all. Then when you go home, you can start to work for the exam. And work. And work.'

'Joseph!'

They both looked up. Afra was running over the grass towards them. Her white T-shirt was covered with dust and her blue trousers were splashed with mud. She arrived, laughing and panting.

'You've made it! That's so brilliant. I thought you'd be stuck on the road someplace and never get here at all. Come and see him before it gets too dark.'

Joseph lifted his eyebrows enquiringly.

'You mean the rhino?'

'Who else? I've been watching him almost all day. I was so longing for you to get here.'

Titus smiled at them.

'Go on then, both of you. I still have work to

do in the office. Be back in our quarters by seven o'clock. Don't stray away from the buildings. It's much too dangerous after dark. There's plenty of big game in this park, and all of it's hungry.'

He walked off. Afra looked at Joseph.

'Are you OK? I mean, did you get to your grandfather's all right? And what did Titus say just now? I guess he felt a little sorry for what he said to you back there, when they were doing the darting. I straightened him out a bit on that.'

'Thank you.' Joseph had been speaking nothing but Kikamba and Swahili for the last day or two and as usual he found English awkward at first. 'Grandfather was good. It is always good with him in the village. And Titus too, he is not so angry now.'

'He was stressed out. Darting rhinos is always kind of a tough job. Omondi was telling me all the things that can go wrong. I mean the vet has to be such a genius, getting the exact balance right for the tranquillizers. Just one little bit of the wrong chemical and bang, you lose your rhino. And it's so dangerous for the guys as well. Uncle Titus said he knew he shouldn't have taken us. He got real nervous when he saw the big fellow starting off up the ravine again, after he thought he was already crashing out.'

She stopped and shook her head, laughing at herself.

'I'm sorry. I promised myself I wouldn't just

talk about rhinos. I want to hear about the village and everything, honestly I do. It's just that I've been with him all day, kind of getting to know him and he's so . . . I don't know . . . so beautiful.'

Joseph grinned at her.

'Afra, you're crazy,' he said. 'Really crazy. You think rhinos are beautiful?'

She nodded emphatically.

'Sure I do. Look, he's only just over there. Come and see him.'

The *boma* was made of split tree trunks rammed deep into the earth and lined with planks to form a good-sized and very strong enclosure. At one side, a covered corridor ran into it, with a heavy gate of thick planks at each end.

'I can't see anything,' said Joseph, disappointed. 'The fence is too high.'

'No, you have to go round the back,' Afra told him. 'Come on.'

Joseph followed her round the side of the *boma*. There were crossbars here against the enclosure wall and they scrambled up onto them. From this vantage point it was easy to look down into the *boma*.

Dusk was falling fast and for a moment Joseph thought the pen was empty. Then he saw that the patch of grey shadow in one corner was in fact the bulk of the rhino. He was standing motionless, his head lowered.

'He looks OK,' said Joseph. 'He's quite calm.'

'Yes, but we'd better keep quiet,' whispered Afra. 'If he gets scared and disturbed he tramples about and tries to charge his way through the walls. He could really hurt himself.'

'He looks smaller,' said Joseph. 'And a little sad.'

He felt uneasy, looking down on the magnificent creature which had taken more than ten men to subdue the day before. It was as if they were taking an unfair advantage.

Something occurred to him.

'He's a black rhino, isn't he?' he said. 'But he doesn't look black. He's just a kind of grey colour, the same as the white rhinos.'

Afra nodded.

'I know. It's kind of confusing. I kept staring at him for ages, trying to figure out if he was just dusty on top, and a real black colour underneath. But Titus told me it doesn't have anything to do with colour because they're all a kind of dark grey. It's about their mouths. "White" comes from the word for "wide" in Afrikaans because they've got wide mouths. The wide-mouthed ones got called "white" and I suppose they just called the others "black" because it's the opposite of white.' She grinned at him. 'Like you and me. White people call us black, but you're a kind of reddish brown and I'm a sort of milky coffee. Weird, isn't it?'

Joseph looked at the rhino's mouth. It was a

little narrower than the other rhinos he'd seen, in Nairobi National Park. It gave him a noble look, somehow, an extra kind of dignity.

'When can he be allowed to go out?' he said.

'I don't know. They have to keep him here to see he hasn't got some sickness that could infect the others and to get him used to the food here. There are all kinds of plants he doesn't know here, and he won't know what to eat. He might get real hungry and try something poisonous. They'll only let him out when he's settled down and really got acquainted with the place, I suppose.'

She leaned further over into the *boma*.

'Do you think he's homesick? He looks a little depressed. Like he was missing his mom or something.'

Joseph smiled.

'Afra, he's a rhino. How can he be depressed?'

'Well, he might be. I mean, we wouldn't know, would we?'

'Maybe he's feeling relieved, because he is safe now and the poachers can't get at him. Anyway, his mother probably got shot years ago, when all those poacher gangs were operating with machine-guns, and all the rhinos in Kenya were practically wiped out.'

Afra sniffed.

'It doesn't mean he doesn't miss his mom just because she died years ago.'

'Listen,' said Joseph severely. 'If you start to ascribe human emotions to a rhino . . .'

Afra's eyebrows flew up and she looked round at Joseph, pursing her lips in a little whistle, as if she was impressed.

'Ascribe?' she said. 'Oh wow. OK, Professor Joseph Mutua. You win. I guess rhinos aren't a bit the same as us. They'd never get to look so pleased with themselves for using a word straight out of the dictionary, anyway.'

He waggled his eyebrows ferociously at her, and she laughed, but then, from the far side of the *boma*, near the rangers' quarters, came a sudden noise.

'What was that?' said Joseph.

'An animal, I guess.' Afra cocked her head to listen. 'Lions hunting, maybe?'

The sound came again.

'That wasn't an animal,' said Joseph, scrambling hastily down off the crossbar. 'It was a person. Come on, Afra, we must go and see!'

4

TWO BRAINS

Joseph and Afra raced across the open ground towards the trees behind the staff quarters. They could hear clearly now that someone was screaming.

Joseph felt himself break out in a prickly sweat. What if it's a leopard or a lion attacking someone, he thought. I haven't even got a spear.

His grandfather's face flashed into his mind for a moment and he made himself run even faster.

He'd outstripped Afra by now. He came round behind the clump of trees and skidded to a halt. A big man was bending over a boy who was lying in the dust. The man was kicking him savagely with heavily booted feet. The boy had stopped screaming. He was whimpering in the high-pitched, helpless voice of someone who knows there's no hope of rescue.

Joseph hesitated for a moment, not knowing what to do, but Afra dashed past him and hurled herself against the big man.

'Stop! Don't! Leave him alone!' she was shouting. 'You'll kill him!'

The man picked Afra up bodily and flung her

away. Luckily she landed on her feet. Joseph was galvanized into action. He rushed at the man himself, tripped up at the last minute and cannoned into him, his head butting hard into the big man's stomach.

The man doubled up, winded. Afra and Joseph launched themselves at him again. The man turned and, still bent over, limped away out of sight.

Joseph and Afra crouched down to look at the boy on the ground. He looked up at them and began struggling to his feet. One eye was already swelling up so fast that it was half closed and blood flowed from a bad cut on his leg. At the same time, Afra and Joseph made a discovery. One of the boy's arms was missing. Only a short stump hung from his left shoulder.

They both helped him to stand. He stood panting, leaning on Joseph for support while Afra bent down to inspect the wound on his leg.

'Hey, this is bad,' she said. 'We need to get Titus's first aid kit for this.'

'Here's my shoulder. Just put your arm around it,' said Joseph. 'Eh! Your face! It's very bad. Can you hop?'

The boy put his hand up to feel his bruised face and winced. He looked round nervously.

'Is he still here? That man?' he said thickly. 'If he comes back he'll kill me for sure.'

'No, no, he's gone,' said Afra reassuringly.

'Come on. We have to get you home. Where do you live?'

The boy didn't answer. He was shaking from head to toe.

'I guess he's in shock.' Afra, who had nursed many wounded animals back to health, was taking charge of the situation. 'We'd better get him back to our place, Joseph.'

Joseph hitched the boy's one arm round his shoulders and put a steady hand on his waist.

'Where is our place?' Joseph said. 'I came only just now.'

'Over there.' Afra nodded towards a pleasant stone house set among trees a little way from the lines of rangers' houses. 'It's the warden's house, but he's away at the moment. It's really good. The animals come all around it at night. Mongooses playing on the grass, and the cutest warthog piglets. I even saw an aardvark last night. My first. They're so shy, I thought I'd be ninety years old before I ever got to see one.'

They were walking slowly now, the boy hobbling between them.

'What's your name?' Joseph asked him. 'And who was that man? Why was he beating you?'

The boy shook his head.

'It's OK,' Afra said quickly. 'You don't have to try and talk. You must be feeling like a boxer's punchball.'

They reached the house.

'Wait here,' said Afra. 'I'll get the kit.'

Joseph helped the boy to sit down in the shade of a big acacia tree. The boy seemed a little better. He smiled shakily up at Joseph and wiped his one hand across his nose, leaving a dusty smear across his face.

Joseph sat down beside him. The boy didn't seem to want to talk. He kept looking anxiously over his shoulder.

'It's OK,' Joseph said reassuringly in Swahili, guessing the boy's thoughts. 'He isn't going to come back. If he does, he'll have to fight me and Afra too.'

But he didn't feel too sure, and when he thought the boy wasn't looking he turned his head uneasily and scanned the thick wooded area behind.

Afra came back at last. She held a white box in one hand and a bowl of water in the other.

'Sorry it took so long,' she said. 'I was looking for Nathan, but he's not around anywhere. I had to hunt all over the place for the first aid stuff.'

'Who's Nathan?' asked Joseph.

'The cook.'

She knelt down and began expertly to wash the boy's wound. Then she opened the first aid kit and hesitated, lifting out a tube of ointment and reading the writing on the side.

The boy watched her anxiously.

'Don't worry,' said Joseph kindly. 'She's treated

many animals for their injuries. They always recover very nicely.'

'Animals?' the boy said. An even more anxious expression crossed his face.

'There,' said Afra at last, rocking back on her heels and looking at her handiwork with a pleased smile.

The boy looked down at himself. A neat bandage was tied around his leg, pink sticking plaster criss-crossed various abrasions on his brown shins and arm, and disinfectant had been dabbed on his face. He smiled for the first time, his dry lips cracking.

'You're thirsty!' said Afra. 'Of course! Shock victims are supposed to have sweet tea.' She looked at Joseph doubtfully. 'I guess I don't know how we'd do that. I mean, I don't know how to work the stove here, or where Nathan keeps the tea or anything.'

Joseph stood up. He'd been feeling redundant and was glad to have something to do.

'Water's OK,' he said. 'Just to drink something is good. Wait here.'

He threw the slops from the basin onto the ground and ran over to a standpipe near the back door. A minute later he was back, the bowl brimming over with clean cool water.

The boy balanced the bowl in his one hand and drank deeply.

'Thank you,' he said shyly.

Afra and Joseph looked at him expectantly.

'I'm Afra,' said Afra after a long pause. 'This is Joseph.'

'I'm . . . my name is . . . Isaac,' said the boy, but everyone calls me One-arm.'

'One-arm?' said Afra indignantly. 'But wouldn't you rather they called you Isaac?'

'Nobody does that,' the boy said. 'It would confuse them.' He drank again, then put the bowl down. 'But I don't see,' he went on in a stronger voice, 'why it's only my arm they look at. I have two of everything else. Two eyes, two legs, two ears, two—'

'Two noses?' said Joseph. 'Two brains?'

They all laughed.

'Yes,' the boy said proudly. 'Maybe I have two brains. I'm first in my class in every subject.'

'In science too?' Joseph was eyeing him with respect. 'You can do chemistry?'

The boy shook his head.

'I'm too young. Chemistry is for the upper classes.'

'Hey.' Afra was packing the medicines back into the first aid kit. 'How would it be if we call you Two-brains? Two for short. What do you think?'

The boy chuckled, turning his battered face from one to the other.

'Two? I like that. Two! Eh! It's better than

44

One-arm, anyway. Better even than Isaac. Yes, it's good. Two!'

'Who was he then, the man who beat you?' said Joseph suddenly, unable to contain his curiosity any longer.

The boy's face closed up again at once.

'I don't know. He is a stranger to me.'

He's lying, Joseph thought. He's too scared to tell.

'Where do you live?' said Afra, frowning at Joseph for distressing her patient.

'Over there.' Two lifted his chin towards the outer fence of the game park that ran behind the warden's house. 'In the village. My father is the headmaster of the school.'

He nodded proudly as he said it.

'You mean you don't live in the rangers' quarters here?' said Afra, puzzled.

Two shook his head.

'My father sent me with a message to his brother,' he said, responding unwillingly to the curiosity in the two avid faces in front of him. 'He works at the main gate. My uncle wasn't there so I – I – the men told me, "Go to the staff quarters. Look for him there." So I was going on my way, and this man, he caught hold of me and he started beating me.'

Afra wrinkled her nose.

'For no reason? He just started in to beat you? What is he, a psychopath?'

'It's all right,' Joseph said gently. 'You don't have to tell us anything. But I think now it's better for you to go home. Look, it's nearly dark.'

'Yes!' Two stood up, staggering a little as he took the weight on his wounded leg. 'My father will be searching for me. But thank you. You have been a brother and a sister for me. I would like very much to see you again.'

'You will.' Afra nodded. 'I have to check up on my patient tomorrow. We'll come to the village to see how you are. Is it far to walk?'

'Not far,' said Two. 'From the main gate the path leads directly up the hill to my village. Good-night! I'll see you tomorrow.'

5

WILDFIRE

Joseph slept well that night, tired out by his long journey. He woke early. He lay still for a while, listening to the curious bubbling song of the nightjar, then, wanting to explore, he crept out of bed, trying not to wake Uncle Titus, who was asleep in the other corner of the room.

He pushed open the outside door and stepped out into the cool dawn. The air shimmered with waking life. Paradise flycatchers swooped and fluttered in the trees overhead, their long streamer tail feathers slicing the air like banners. A pair of shy waterbuck, their ears pricked, observed him nervously from the edge of the clearing, and a troop of baboons, who had spent the night in a nearby tree, were climbing down in a leisurely manner, or sitting on the ground, looking round at the new day with bright, intelligent eyes. They were used to humans and took no notice of him.

'Hi! You're up too. Isn't it great here? It's just like someone waved a magic wand.'

He turned round. Afra was coming out through the door behind him. She stood still for a moment, her head thrown back, looking up into the trees where a hornbill had just landed, his great red beak standing out against the green leaves like a long curved fruit.

'Are you coming?' she said. 'I'm going to see Wildfire.'

Joseph looked puzzled.

'Who's Wildfire?'

'The rhino, of course. Didn't I tell you? That's what Omondi calls him. He says he's the wildest fieriest rhino he's ever caught.'

They began to run off across the grass.

'Joseph! Afra! Where are you going?'

They turned round. Titus was standing in the door, blinking sleepily at them and buttoning up his shirt.

'Only to see Wildfire,' said Afra.

'Good idea. I'll come with you. Just let me wash my face at least.'

He disappeared and came back a few moments later, then began to stride so fast across the grass towards the *boma* that Joseph and Afra had to run to keep up with him.

They climbed up onto the crossbar and hung over the fence looking down at the rhino, which was feeding peacefully from a pile of leaves.

'Extraordinary creatures,' said Titus ruminatively. 'Full of contradictions. They're so blind, but so quick to sense their enemies. And they're big and heavy but they run as fast as the wind and turn as quickly as a cat. And they're so ugly to look at, but they carry on their heads the most valuable animal product in the world.'

'It doesn't look valuable at all,' said Afra, squinting against the rising sun to get a better view of the rhino's two chipped and scarred horns.

'And yet it sells here for $300 a kilo, and you must pay 2000 US dollars for a kilo of powdered rhino horn medicine in China,' said Titus.

'But how can it be a medicine?' said Joseph. 'It's just a piece of horn.'

'Oh, there's some small benefit, to reduce fever,' Titus said. 'But aspirin works much better.'

'I don't get it.' Afra's eyes were snapping crossly. 'I don't get how anyone can shoot an animal like Wildfire just to steal his horn. It's so wicked. It's so evil!'

Titus smiled at her.

'You've never been poor, Afra. If you have children to feed and no work, and someone offers you many hundreds of dollars to hunt a rhino, and take his horn, you'll be tempted to accept. $100 is a lot of money here. $1000 is a fortune.'

Afra glared at him. She drew a deep breath.

'I would never, never hurt an animal. I would lay down my life for a rhino.'

She had spoken more shrilly than she had intended and the rhino began to move his head restlessly from side to side. Gingerly, trying not to make a noise, the three of them clambered down from the crossbar and began to walk slowly back towards the house.

'I'd shoot any poacher that crossed my path,' Afra went on. 'They're just murderers! Monsters! They're sadistic, barbaric—'

'Hey, hey!' Titus held up his hands placatingly. 'Poachers are people too. They're wrong. They're criminals and we want to stop them. But they do what they do for a reason.'

'What reason?' cried Afra passionately. 'Who cares about their reasons?'

'I do.' Titus spoke feelingly too. 'You have to understand your enemies if you want to fight them. It's not always so simple.'

'Yes it is. There's right and there's wrong, and poachers are wrong,' said Afra positively.

Uncle Titus didn't seem to hear her.

'Before,' he said, 'people and animals, they lived together in Africa. They were part of each other. People hunted a little just for food, when they needed it.'

'Or like Grandfather,' said Joseph. 'When a lion or a leopard attacked his goats, he used to kill them with his spear.'

'OK, but it was different then,' said Afra. 'No one made money out of animals then.'

'But they do now,' said Titus. 'Rhino horn and ivory from elephants' tusks, these have suddenly become some of the most valuable things in the world. People who are poor think, "We'll just get hold of some of this stuff and we'll be rich, rich beyond our dreams!" '

Joseph was frowning, thinking things out.

'If the rhinos are so valuable, Uncle Titus, soon the poachers will kill all of them. They'll become extinct!'

'No!' cried Afra. 'You have to protect them! Put up better fences! Get more guards!'

'Fences can come down,' said Titus. 'They won't stay there for ever. And guards are only human beings themselves. Some of them might be tempted by the money too. You must think about the future, and the future's with the people, with the way they feel about things. If all the animals are locked away inside parks, the people outside won't remember how their grandfathers used to live alongside those old rhinos, when they were running about freely, huffing and puffing through the bush. "Why should we bother?" they'll say. "Why should we protect them?" '

Afra slammed one fist into the other palm.

'I don't believe this! You mean we shouldn't bother to guard the rhinos? So the poachers come and get them all and we let them go extinct? Uncle Titus, that's . . . that's *immoral*!'

Titus frowned and Joseph held his breath. Titus was used to the African way, to being treated with respect by younger people. If Joseph had dared to speak to him like that Titus would have been furious.

She doesn't mean to be rude, he urged his uncle silently. It's just what she's like when she really, really cares about something.

It was as if Titus had heard him. His frown smoothed itself away.

'Of course we will always need guards and fences round some of our parks,' he said, and his only rebuke was his quiet dignity. 'But people, ordinary Kenyan people, are our best security. We have to show them that the animals can be good for them too. Why shouldn't they have a share in the prosperity the parks bring? If they do, the animals will be more precious to them when they're alive than if they're killed.'

'You mean if the park pays people around here some of the money they get from tourists?' said Afra. She was simmering down as quickly as a boiled kettle when it's been taken off the fire.

Joseph grimaced.

'Afra, sometimes you think without using your head at all. Can't you hear them all saying, "Hey, listen, brothers and sisters, they're handing out money at Nakuru!" There would be a stampede, like when the wildebeest are running!'

Afra made a face at him.

'OK then, clever. What would you do?'

Joseph thought for a minute, then he shrugged.

'I don't know. I don't think there's an answer.'

'There might be an answer,' said Uncle Titus. 'Money's not the only thing people want. They want schools for their kids and clinics and proper roads. If some of the park money is spent on that, they'll make sure the parks do well and the animals are looked after and the tourists keep coming.'

'That's . . . yes, that's really good!' Afra turned a suddenly enthusiastic face towards him. 'It would mean that if the poachers come and try to sneak into the park, the people around here would tell them to get lost instead of helping them.'

'That's right.' Uncle Titus nodded. 'They'll be good neighbours for the rhino. And without local help, what can the poachers do? Not so much. It's not so easy for them.'

They had reached the house now. Titus looked at his watch.

'I'm sorry,' he said. 'I have so much work to do. I would like to drive you round the park to see the animals but it must wait until this evening. You'll have to stay around the house today. You know you mustn't wander around in the park on foot? It's very dangerous. I don't want to be the man to tell your father, Afra, if you're chased by a buffalo or eaten by a lion. He'd never let me take you away with Joseph again.'

Afra grinned.

'You wouldn't be able to take me away with you again if I'd been eaten by a lion. Anyway, Prof probably wouldn't take it in,' she said. 'He'd be too busy with his old bits of pottery and bones and stuff. Actually, we weren't planning on going into the park this morning. But is it OK if we go out of it? We want to go see Two.'

'Two?' asked Titus.

'We told you last night, Uncle Titus,' said Joseph. 'The boy with one arm who was being beaten up.'

'Oh yes.' Titus had clearly dismissed Two from his mind. 'That's good. Go to the village. It's not far from the gate. You'll find some new friends among the kids there, I'm sure.' He looked at his watch again. 'I'll see you this afternoon. Don't get into trouble!'

Joseph and Afra grabbed a quick breakfast and made their way back to the main gate. The two guards were friendly now. They knew who the children were.

'You are going to the village?' one of them said. 'Tell those village kids, "If you come back in here looking for firewood, we will tell your fathers. You will be punished." '

'The kids come into the park for firewood?' said Afra.

'Every day! They are too mischievous. One day a big leopard in a ranger's uniform will catch them and eat them,' one of the guards said, laughing.

Afra smiled back at him, but as they walked on up the track towards the village, she saw that Joseph was frowning.

'What's up with you? Seen the bogeyman or something?'

'Yes, perhaps I have. Did you look inside the gatehouse?'

Afra shook her head.

'There was a man there. He was standing beside the door but when he saw us, immediately he turned to show me only his back.'

'So what? Maybe he didn't like the look of us. I mean, we're not Barbie and Ken exactly, are we? At least, I guess if I grew a whole lot taller and dyed my hair blond and painted myself pink all over I'd be kind of like Barbie, but you . . .'

'Afra, will you shut your mouth? I think the guy I saw was the man who was beating Two.'

'No!' Afra was silenced immediately. 'But what was he doing at the gatehouse?'

'Perhaps he's a friend of one of the guards. Do you know what I think? I think probably Two was taking firewood from out of the park, illegally, and the man caught him and that is why he beat him.'

Afra shook her head.

'No. He was too violent. Too vicious. There was something else going on. It was like the guy wanted to actually murder him. Maybe Two will be less scared today and tell us.'

They had reached the first house in the village now. A girl was coming down the path towards them, leading a small flock of goats.

Joseph greeted her politely in Swahili.

'We're looking for Isaac,' he said.

The girl shook her head.

'One-arm,' said Joseph reluctantly.

The girl nodded and pointed to a small house beside a banana plantation, where chickens were scratching about in the dust.

Joseph and Afra walked up to it. Joseph coughed quietly to announce their presence. At once they heard someone inside and Two came to the door.

'You are here!' he said, beaming from ear to ear. 'You came!'

Joseph and Afra both drew in their breath. Two's face, which had looked battered enough the night before, was positively grotesque this morning. It was horribly swollen and his battered right eye was an angry bloodshot red. He came out into the open.

'You look awful,' said Afra frankly.

'I know.' Two squatted down by the door and the others followed suit. 'But I feel well. It hurts only a little now. And my leg is fine too, if I don't touch it. You are my good, good friends. You have saved me.'

'You don't think that guy was going to kill you, do you?' said Afra.

'Maybe no, maybe yes.' Two picked up a couple of stones and began tossing them up in the air and catching them on the back of his only hand.

'But why?' Joseph burst out. 'Listen. I think I saw him this morning, by the gatehouse. The man turned his back when he saw me, but he was the same one, I'm sure of it.'

Two looked at them, his one open eye assessing them shrewdly.

'You are my friends,' he said at last. 'I think I can trust you.'

'Of course you can,' began Afra indignantly, but Joseph put a hand on her arm to quieten her.

'I wanted to tell you yesterday,' said Two, 'but I was very much afraid. That man, his name is Chege. Once he worked here in the park, but he lost his job. I don't know why. He was very angry for that. He still has friends here, with the guards. He comes and sits with them and they talk together. He's nice to those men, but to me, yesterday, he was very terrible, like a devil. I found out something bad about him. That's why he threatened me. He told to me, "If you tell another person about me, I'll kill you." I believe him. I think he will kill me. That's why I'm afraid.'

'Don't tell us, then, if it's that bad,' said Afra. 'But you can trust us, you know. We wouldn't tell a soul.'

Two let the stones fall off his hand onto the ground.

'OK,' he said. 'I'll tell you. Chege, he is a thief. I was coming to the park last night for . . . well . . .'

'To get firewood?' said Joseph.

Two looked embarrassed.

'Yes. I know it is not legal, but my mother sent me to look for it, and it is not easy to find firewood outside the park.'

'Hey, wait a minute! You can't take stuff out of the park!' Afra said, with a yelp of disapproval. 'If all the trees are cut down, what will happen to the animals?'

Joseph nudged her so hard she almost toppled over.

'Go on,' he said to Two.

'I know it is bad,' Two said defensively. 'But it is only for this year. We have planted some trees for fuel. They will be ready for cutting soon. Then we will not come to take firewood again.'

'Yes, but what about Chege?' said Joseph impatiently.

'I was going quietly, quietly behind the gatehouse,' Two went on, 'to leave the park. I had already gathered some wood and I had thrown it over the fence to where I could collect it later. So I was trying to get out again. And then I saw him.'

'Saw who? Saw what?' Joseph and Afra were eagerly following every word.

'I saw Chege. He was in the gatehouse. The guards were talking to the driver of a car that was coming in through the big gates. Chege had gone inside and he had opened the drawer where the guards keep the money. It is the money of the entrance by the tourists to the park. I suppose he knew how to work the lock because he used to work here himself. He was taking some big notes and putting them in his pocket. He looked up and saw me looking at him. At once he ran out and began to chase me. He caught me and then you came, my dear friends, and saved me.'

'So that's it!' Joseph nodded slowly. 'You were right. The man's a thief. If Uncle Titus knew . . .'

'No, no! Please, you must not tell! You have promised me!' Two waved his hand in agitation. 'Chege will discover it. And then my father will find out, and he will try to fight Chege because Chege beat me. But my father is not so strong. His heart is not good now. If he tries to fight with Chege, I will be too afraid.'

'You mean you didn't even tell your mom and dad what happened to you last night?' said Afra admiringly. 'Wow. I couldn't have kept quiet like that. I'd have told everybody, including the birds in the trees.'

'What did you tell them then?' asked Joseph.

Two grinned.

'I told them I climbed a tree to get a dead branch, and it broke, and I fell down and a leopard chased me,' he said.

They all laughed.

Then Afra said, 'OK, Two. You win. We can't go to Titus yet. No one would believe a kid like you anyway. We have to watch the man ourselves, that's all, and see if we can get some more evidence.'

'That is not the whole story.'

Two spoke quietly, and Afra crouched down again to listen.

'I have seen Chege yesterday morning in the village. There was a car with two men in it. Chege was talking to them through the window. I think he has some bad friends.'

Joseph looked at him doubtfully.

'Why do you think they're bad?'

'I have seen these men before. They came in the bad times, years ago, when there were many poachers around Nakuru.'

'Poachers!' exclaimed Afra sharply.

'I don't know for sure that they are poachers,' Two went on, 'but those two, they used to come from Nairobi to visit Chege. I think they were his relatives, maybe. They used to drink in the bars around here. But I was only a little kid then. Maybe I'm wrong.'

'Maybe you're right,' said Joseph seriously.

'Surely there can't be poachers here?' said Afra. 'Not after everything Uncle Titus was telling us. Anyway, the park's so well guarded. It would be impossible. At least . . .' Her voice tailed off.

'Yes.' Joseph nodded. 'I know what you're

thinking. If they had help from inside, someone who knew the park well, who could get them inside secretly and show them where the rhinos are, maybe they could do it.'

'But the park's so big,' objected Afra, though her voice was uncertain. 'They'd never find a rhino there. And they wouldn't go for Wildfire. His *boma*'s too near the staff quarters. Someone would hear them.'

'It is not so difficult to find a rhino,' said Two. 'There are many of them, more than sixty even, if you count the white rhinos and the black rhinos together. I can see some myself every day. They like to go to the same places every day. I know somewhere, a good place, where you can watch them easily.'

'Where?' said Afra eagerly.

'It's a place like a picnic spot on the top of a cliff.' Two pointed up the hill above the village. 'The tourists go there. It is safe for them there to go outside of their cars because the rhinos, they stay down below. The tourist guides allow them to walk about.'

'They're lucky,' said Joseph. 'I'd like to go there.'

'You would like to go there?' Two looked pleased. 'I can take you. There is a place where it's possible to go under the fence.'

'No thanks,' said Afra. 'It's all electrified. You

might touch it by mistake. I don't want to get fried.'

Two grinned.

'You would not get fried, or even roasted, or boiled. There is a place I can show you that only the kids know about. The ground is not flat there. There is a hole under the fence. It is easy to get through it.'

Afra and Joseph looked at each other.

'Titus would be furious if he found out,' said Afra.

Joseph pursed his lips.

'He didn't say we couldn't go into the park. He only said we shouldn't wander around inside.'

'How do you expect us to move around once we're inside, then?' demanded Afra. 'Roller blades? Hang glider? Covered wagon? Anyway, it's too dangerous. Like he said, I don't want him to be taking my half-eaten remains home to Prof.'

Two had been following her with difficulty.

'It is not dangerous in that part,' he said. 'The rhinos don't go there in the morning, and there are no buffalo or lions at this side. They're all down near the water. And the safe place is very close to the fence. Even we can see the tourists sometimes from the other side. We don't have to walk far until we reach there.'

'Oh,' said Afra. 'Well, in that case, I guess, maybe . . .'

Joseph stood up.

'Come on,' he said. 'What are we waiting for?'

6

THE RHINO CALF

Two had been right. It turned out to be easy, easier in fact than Two himself had expected, to get into the park. As the three of them walked up the hill towards the fence, they passed the back service entrance. A truck full of building materials destined for the tourist lodge had pulled up, and the driver was leaning out of his cab calling for the ranger to open the gate.

The ranger knew the truck driver. He came running out of his hut, shouting a greeting, the keys to the gates in his hand. He opened the gate in the outer fence, then went across the narrow strip of land to unlock the inner gate.

Two looked at the truck through narrowed eyes, then he grinned.

'Follow me!' he whispered.

He darted across to the far side of the truck, away from the ranger, who was swapping funny stories with the driver and laughing uproariously.

Two put his finger to his lips.

'Wait!' he hissed.

At last the truck began moving again and, hidden from the view of the driver and ranger, the children trotted alongside it, through the double gates and into the park.

'That was so easy,' said Afra, looking at Two with a mixture of respect and surprise.

Joseph said nothing. He was anxious. If they were caught and Uncle Titus heard about this he'd be in real trouble. He'd feel he'd let his uncle down.

There wasn't time to worry though. Two was already leading the way through the long grass under the cover of the scattered acacia trees. People had clearly come this way many times before. The path was well-worn.

They came out of the trees suddenly and found themselves near the edge of a steep cliff, which fell away in a sheer drop to the lake hundreds of metres below.

Joseph gasped with delight and surprise. They were looking down into a perfect small world, a scene untouched by the hand of man. The lake, stretching a long way down to the wooded fringe at its far end, glittered in the morning sunlight. A wide plain of golden grass lay to one side, and even from this height it was easy to see the animals, a herd of grazing buffalo, another of zebra, a few skittish gazelle, their black and white rumps flashing as they bolted from some unseen danger in the grass.

'What's that pink stuff on the lake?' whispered Afra.

65

'They're flamingos, aren't they?' said Joseph, looking across at Two, who nodded in confirmation. 'There must be millions of them down there. Why are you whispering?'

'I don't know. I guess . . . I guess . . .' Afra hesitated. 'Oh, it's just so beautiful. Like humans have never been here before.'

Two was scanning the plain below, his practised eyes screwed up against the bright morning light.

'There,' he said, pointing. 'Rhino. Maybe they are males. I cannot see from here. Usually a female and her calf are in that place in the morning. But I cannot see the calf today.'

Joseph and Afra craned forward, following his finger. Joseph could see them now, three dark shapes moving slowly through the grass. He felt a little disappointed.

'They're a long way from here,' he said. 'We can't see them easily.'

'You want them to come here?' Two chuckled. 'You want them to charge up and chase you?'

Joseph turned to smile at him.

'No, of course—' he began. Then he froze, and his jaw dropped.

'What's the matter?' said Afra, turning herself to look at whatever he had seen. 'Oh, wow!'

A rhino was walking quietly along the path towards them, her grey body dappled in the sunlight filtering through the trees. She was no more than forty metres away.

'Freeze! Don't move!' Joseph mouthed at the other two.

The rhino's sight was bad, he knew. She'd only see them if they moved. But her sense of smell was excellent and her hearing was good too. She had another great advantage. Her little watchman, an oxpecker, was on her back. He rode the rhino like a miniature jockey, his small red body swaying as she walked, his scarlet bill bobbing up and down. If he raised the alarm, the rhino might take fright and charge. She'd stampede them at terrifying speed, and dodging around wouldn't help much. She'd be able to turn in no time and would be on them in a second.

Joseph's mind was working overtime. Which way was the wind blowing? What were the chances of the rhino getting their scent? He tried to feel the currents of air on his skin. A vague memory of something he'd learned at school came back to him. Air rose when it was heated. As the morning sun warmed the air on the plain below, surely it would rise, billowing up over the edge of the cliff, wafting towards the rhino and carrying their scent with it? And if she smelled them ... Then, with a spurt of relief, he felt the suggestion of coolness on his face. A tiny breeze was blowing the *other* way, towards the cliff top, not away from it.

Afra gave a little gasp and quickly suppressed it. Joseph could see why. A small grey copy of the rhino was trotting along behind her. The female rhino had a calf.

They'd been coming on inexorably, closer and closer, but suddenly they stopped. Joseph's stomach fell with a sickening thud. Had the rhino sensed their presence? Was she getting ready to charge at them? Then he saw the calf drop down into the grass and roll over on his side, as if he wanted to play. The mother lowered her head, weighed down by its heavy horn, towards him.

The baby scrambled awkwardly to his feet again and, nosing his way around his mother's long side, he thrust his head between her back legs, searching for a nipple. He began to suckle, his little tail flickering contentedly across his fat rump.

In spite of his anxiety, Joseph was filled with wonder.

They have always been here, he thought. They are a part of Africa. A part of me.

Beside him, Afra and Two sat like stones, gazing in silence.

The mother stood for a long time, patiently waiting for her calf to finish his feed. Once or twice she twitched an ear or lifted a heavy foot and stamped it down again. Then, from below, she heard an alien sound. A minibus was approaching up the steep slope from the plain below. With a grunt she began to move, picking up her great feet and plopping them down again onto the ground with surprising delicacy. She was making for the cover of the trees. With her calf behind her, she disappeared, melting suddenly away into the shadows, in the opposite direction from the path.

'That . . . was . . . incredible!' Afra let out her breath in a rush. 'It was just the most amazing thing I ever saw! I wish Tom had seen them. They'd have blown his mind.'

Joseph said nothing. He was still seeing the rhino and her calf in his mind's eye, still feeling a strange awe, a strange peace.

'Come, quick,' said Two, pulling at Joseph's sleeve. 'The minibus is coming. They mustn't find us here.'

They jumped up and began retreating after Two down the path towards the gate again. The minibus was close now. They could even hear the noisy talking and laughter of the people in it.

They stood hidden among the trees to watch it. It was white and open-topped. About ten tourists were standing up in it, holding binoculars and cameras up to their faces.

'I don't get it,' said Afra. 'Do they really think they're going to see any animals when they're making such a noise?'

'They are tourists,' said Two with a shrug. 'They don't know animals. Come, let's go.'

The minibus had pulled up and the tourists were spilling out of it.

'Look at that!' said Afra disgustedly, as one of them, a young girl, drained a drink can and threw it into the bushes.

She looked as if she was about to march out and give the girl a piece of her mind.

'Afra, no,' said Joseph. 'Come on. We mustn't be found here. It's better for us to go.'

'Ugh, and they're smoking too,' said Afra, as the first acrid whiff of tobacco smoke assailed her nostrils. 'That's so gross. I mean the air here smells so sweet. And anyway, they could easily start a fire.'

'Come on,' said Joseph again, tugging at her arm.

Reluctantly she turned, and together they followed Two, who was already disappearing as silently as a shadow up the path towards the gate.

7

A GAME OF FOOTBALL

Joseph looked round uneasily. They'd been wrong to come into the park, he knew that. The rhino had given him an awful fright. If they'd made one little sound, or if the rhino had come a bit closer, or if the wind had got up, she'd have become aware of them. She'd have been even more edgy with a calf to worry about, and she'd probably have charged. They'd have been trampled to death, or they'd have gone straight over the edge of the cliff.

He'd been wrong to trust Two. If the rhino had come up here, to this remote part of the park, what other animals might be lurking nearby? There could be lions. There could easily be leopards in the trees.

And how are we going to get out of here? he thought anxiously. We can't expect another truck to come along at the right moment. They probably only go through once or twice a day.

The fence was in sight now. It looked impossibly high and forbidding.

We can't climb over that, thought Joseph. We'd never make it.

Ahead of him, Two had reached the inner fence already. He was walking along it, looking carefully at the ground as he went.

Suddenly he stopped and pointed.

'Here,' he said to the others. 'Here is the place.'

Afra and Joseph looked over his shoulder. They could see now that some thick bushes, growing on each side of the fence, were concealing a dip that ran right under the fence from one side to the other. The lower branches had been craftily weighted down with stones so that the dip would be hard to see, unless you knew just where to look for it.

Two began moving the stones, taking care not to break the branches. He used his one hand deftly, and had clearly done this many times before. It was obvious that people had wriggled under the fence here many times, and had been careful to cover their tracks.

Joseph bent down and looked under the wire. The idea of a massive electric shock was scary, but he could see that there was really plenty of space. As long as they were careful, they were in no danger of being electrocuted.

Two was still talking. He looked back over his shoulder at Joseph and Afra.

'The rhino gave me a fright. Aiee!' he said. 'I was not expecting such a thing. It is my first time to see a rhino in that place.'

'I had a big fright, too,' said Joseph drily.

'I wouldn't have missed it for the world,' breathed Afra. 'Hey, do you want a hand with those stones?'

She stopped, embarrassed, realizing that she might have chosen a more tactful way of putting it, but Two didn't seem to notice.

'It's OK,' he said, releasing the last one. 'I can do it.'

The branches of the bush sprang up and Joseph and Afra could see now that the hollow under the fence was quite deep. Two bent down to wriggle under it. Joseph and Afra bent down too, ready to follow him into the no man's land between the inner and the outer fence. Two was almost through to the other side when he suddenly stopped, and Joseph, who had started to crawl down into the dip behind him, nearly bumped into him.

'What's wrong?' he said.

'Something strange is here,' said Two, who was carefully studying a patch of bare earth on the far side of the fence. He moved forward carefully, trying not to disturb the dusty ground. 'Look. There are tracks.'

Joseph, who had felt his back tingle with fear and anticipation in case he accidentally touched the electric wire, had made it under the fence now, and Afra was crawling through after him. Joseph had to admit to a sense of relief. Although there was still the outer fence to tackle he felt safer already. He'd been scared back there. He looked down to the ground where Two was pointing.

There was a confusion of marks in the bare patch of dust but he could make out the old prints of children's feet, the toes clearly outlined. There was something, too, that could be a small bird's foot, with claws spreading out as if from one slender leg. But planted right in the middle was the unmistakable print of a man's trainer, the corrugations of the sole fresh and clearly outlined.

Two was looking up and down along the wide strip of land between the two fences.

'I don't understand,' he said worriedly. 'It is only children who know this place, me and my friends. Who does the foot belong to?'

Joseph looked round too. Low branches hung over the inner fence. The leaves were stirring slightly in the breeze. A moment ago they'd looked normal, but now they seemed sinister, as if someone might be hiding in them, watching.

'Let's go,' he said.

Two was putting in place again the stones left ready on this side of the fence, holding the branches down so neatly that it was almost impossible to tell where the dip was. Now he set off slowly across the wide strip of ground towards the outer fence, looking down at the grass and frowning. Even Joseph could see that someone had come this way, someone heavier than a child, whose weight had broken down the brittle grass stems.

It was easier to see the way out under the outer fence. Dead bushes had been piled roughly against it, as if the last person to come this way had been in a hurry. It took no more than a minute for Two to pull them apart and for the three of them to scramble under the wire.

Everything seemed so ordinary outside the fence that Joseph could hardly believe how different it had been inside. In there, the grass had been long and lush. Out here, it was nibbled down to a smooth velvet by the village goats. Inside, great animals roamed free, the air was filled with the song of wild birds and the only humans were tourists who, stranger even than the animals they had come to see, drove around in their steely vehicles, twittering like starlings. Here, outside the fence, the animals lived at man's behest, dogs, cows and goats at the beck and call of humans, while of all the birds it was the rooster's strident call that he could hear most clearly. As for the people, there was nothing strange about them. They were just farmers and their families. In fact he could see two perfectly ordinary boys coming towards them now, up the hill from the village.

'Don't speak of the footprint,' Two urged the others in a low voice as the boys came closer. 'I must think what it means. And remember, don't speak of Chege.'

The boys ran up the last few metres towards them. They looked curiously at Joseph and Afra.

'*Jambo*,' they said politely. 'You are welcome.'

They sat for a while, too shy to say anything, then one of them spoke to Two in a low voice.

'It is time for our football practice,' he said. 'We are all waiting for you.'

Two put up a hand to his battered head.

'I can't today,' he said. 'It's my head. It has started to ache again. And my leg also, it does not feel good.'

Afra looked at him, shocked.

'Oh, Two! I don't know how we could be so selfish. You're supposed to take it easy after you get a bang on the head. We shouldn't have dragged you off with us like that.'

'No, no, it is not so serious,' said Two hurriedly. 'But I cannot play football well today.'

'But we have the big match next week,' one of the boys said. 'We have to practise. You could just be in goal, maybe.'

'One-arm in goal!' the second boy said, mockingly. 'What are you thinking of? He couldn't stop anything.'

'Why couldn't he?' said Afra hotly. 'Two could do more with one arm than most guys could with three, I bet.'

Two frowned sharply at Afra, then looked down, embarrassed.

'Two?' The two boys looked at each other. 'Who is Two?'

'It is what they call me,' mumbled Two. 'I like it. It is better than One-arm, anyway.'

'It's short for Two-brains,' said Joseph. He saw that Two was still looking uncomfortable. 'I could be goalie,' he said diffidently. 'Just for today, for your practice.'

The two boys smiled delightedly.

'Man, that is the best idea,' one of them said. 'Let us go.'

Joseph looked at Two and Afra.

'Sorry,' he said. 'I'll come and find you later.'

'I'm going back to Two's house with him,' said Afra firmly. 'I want to make sure he's all right.'

'No, please, it is not necessary.' Afra's mothering was clearly irritating Two and he looked at Joseph for support.

'Leave him alone, Afra,' said Joseph crossly. 'He's OK. Come and watch the game.'

'Watch the game? Oh, how fascinating. Thanks a bundle,' said Afra, but she followed the others as they turned and ran down the hill towards the patch of flat rough ground just outside the village.

A cheer rose from the waiting gang of boys as they ran up. The play area was much smaller than a real football pitch, no more, in fact, than an area of open ground between thorny hedges where the dry earth looked too thin for cultivation. But

Joseph felt excited. He hadn't had a good game of football for ages.

Someone tossed the ball into the middle and Joseph bent down to scoop it up. It was home-made, a compressed mass of old plastic bags tied round with string. He suppressed a superior smile.

I can show them a thing or two, he thought confidently. I'll show these kids how we play football in Nairobi.

The game began. Joseph stood at his gaol, a space between two sticks roughly hammered into the ground, and waited, his arms folded. Then suddenly, out of the blue, the ball came at him, a perfect shot, creaming up and over the defenders' heads.

Too late he lunged for it, but it landed with a solid thud squarely behind the goalposts.

Embarrassed, he ran back to retrieve it. The scorer was punching the air, cheering and doing a victory roll.

Joseph lobbed the ball back to the centre of the pitch and hunched himself over, on his guard now.

The play was fast and good. Some of the boys were clumsy, but one or two ran like cheetahs. The ball seemed to be attracted to their feet as if by magnets and they dribbled it with a sureness he had rarely seen, accommodating their moves to every rut and boulder that littered the crude pitch.

On his mettle now, Joseph settled down to do

his best. He was aware of Two and Afra sitting on a mound, talking and watching. Afra had never seen him play football before. He wanted to impress her. Out of the corner of his eye, he could see a few of the village men, watching from a distance, and a couple of young girls, pausing on their way up the track. Not far away, a white car was driving up the hill. He blanked everything out, not wishing to be distracted.

His confidence, which had plummeted after the first disaster, was rising again, and a spectacular save, cheered enthusiastically by his team, gave him a glow of pleasure.

He remembered the African goalies he'd seen on TV when he'd watched the last World Cup. They'd savoured their triumph at the moment of a goal kick, waving the defenders to the right positions, then bouncing the ball a couple of times while they were preparing for the kick. He was about to do the same, but he remembered just in time that the home-made ball couldn't bounce. He held it out in front of his chest, made a short, fierce run and gave it a superb kick, allowing his anchoring leg to leave the ground at the same time in a spectacular hop.

He watched the ball rise higher and higher, then saw that the other players were all standing still. Something was wrong. The ball was going too far, too fast. It was curving up in a perfect trajectory towards the white car, which had pulled up now at the far end of the pitch. Three men were getting out of it.

Joseph's heart gave a sickening thud. One of the men was Chege.

8

ON GUARD

There was something menacing in the way that Chege was looking round at the group of boys.

He's looking for Two, thought Joseph. He wants to shut him up properly.

He glanced swiftly towards the bank where Two and Afra had been sitting a few moments before. They'd disappeared.

He'd better not see me, thought Joseph. He'll realize I've been with Two. He'll guess Two's told us about the money. He'll want to silence us all.

He wanted to turn and run, but made himself move slowly and unobtrusively instead, edging round the side of the pitch towards the nearest house.

He bolted the last few metres, desperate to be out of sight, and found that Two and Afra had taken refuge in the same place.

'Did he see you? Did he recognize you?' said Two urgently.

'I don't think so,' panted Joseph. 'What do we do now?'

Raised voices were coming from the pitch. Cautiously, Joseph looked round the side of the house.

The ball appeared to have hit the car and one of the men was holding it up angrily and shouting at the boys.

'Time to back off, I guess,' Afra said quietly. 'Where do we go now, Two?'

'Not to my house,' Two said, licking his lips nervously. 'Chege is looking for me perhaps. It will not be hard for him. Everyone can tell him where the boy with one arm lives. He will go to my house first. We must go higher up, outside the village, where there are fields and some places to hide behind the hedges.'

He was moving already, stumbling over the loose stones in the alleyway between the houses. He darted across the main track through the village, trying to keep out of sight. Afra and Joseph followed him.

It was just as well that Two, who had been born in the village, knew every corner of it. He led the others so well that they emerged at the top end having come face to face only with one old lady, who peered at them unseeingly through her half-blind eyes, and a startled toddler, who let out a squeak as they dashed towards him, then sat down suddenly, crying, in the dust.

They dropped into the welcome shade of a clump of young saplings.

'No one will come here,' said Two. 'But if they come we can see them from afar, and just go to another place.'

'OK, but maybe we ought to make some kind of plan,' said Afra. 'I mean, we can't just stay here and do nothing. What if Two's right? I mean if those guys are poachers, we can't sit around here all day like three stuffed dummies and let them go on and poach our rhinos. We have to try and stop them.'

'But poachers don't hunt in the middle of the day,' said Joseph. 'They always work at night.'

'Not always.' Two shook his head. 'The park is not so big. You could easily hear the sound of a gun at night and the rangers would come quickly. But in the daytime the sound of shooting is not heard so easily.'

'Yes, I suppose you're right,' nodded Joseph. 'Listen, even from here you can hear the banging of the workmen who are making the road. You wouldn't notice a shot so easily.' He paused. 'But what can we do? We don't even know that these men *are* poachers. Without any proof, who'll believe us if we tell our suspicions?'

'But we have to *do* something,' burst out Afra. 'At this very moment those ... those *murderers* might be tracking down that mother and her calf.'

Two chuckled.

'But the poachers are still in the village. They will not find any rhino there. If one comes, believe me, we will see everyone run away very quickly.'

Joseph nodded.

'That's true. But why are they down there? Why are they showing their faces at all?'

'They are from Nairobi,' Two said, shrugging his thin shoulders. 'Maybe they think that we are just poor stupid country people here, and we are so admiring them because they have a car. Maybe they think the people here will help them.'

'What if they get lucky,' said Afra, 'and some of the villagers do help them?'

Two shook his head decisively.

'They will not. Before, some of our people, when they were hungry, they took animals from the park for their meat and they also helped the poachers of rhino. But the villagers, they are working now for the park. They are gaining too many good things from it. They will listen to these guys when they ask questions, and smile and say "Yes", and "No", and "We don't know", or maybe they will give them the wrong answers.'

'They wouldn't turn them in though, to the park rangers?' said Afra hopefully.

Two shook his head again.

'They would be too much scared. These people, they must have guns for shooting at the rhino and they are not afraid to use them for people also.'

Joseph felt a tightness in his throat.

'OK,' he said. 'So it's up to us. We have to watch them, to get the proof and to stop them if we can. It's a good place here. We can see every path that leads away from the village. They can't leave it without us seeing them.'

There was a short silence. Then Afra said in a small voice, 'Try to stop them? Poachers armed with guns?'

'You said yesterday you'd lay down your life for an animal,' said Joseph, unable to resist the temptation of teasing her.

Afra gulped.

'I guess I just didn't think it would be so soon.'

'It's all right,' Two said patronizingly. 'You are a girl. You do not need to come with us. This is a man's job.'

Afra looked at him indignantly.

'Are you telling me that you think that just because I'm a girl I'm not every bit as brave as you are?'

Joseph whistled under his breath.

'Be careful, Two. You don't know what this girl is like.'

But Two was laughing.

'No, I think you are very brave. But this is how you are to me. I have only one arm, and because of this I think you like to pretend that you are my owner and I am your little animal pet.'

'That's so unfair! I don't!' began Afra indignantly. Then she stopped and bit her lip.

'OK, OK.' Joseph was the only one still watching the village but he turned to the other two and held up his hands for peace. 'We haven't got time to quarrel. The job we have to do is too important.'

'I cannot quarrel with you,' said Two, grinning at Afra. 'You saved me from Chege.'

She shook her head shamefacedly and smiled back.

'I guess you're right. I was kind of patronizing. I got a little carried away, maybe. Just shut me up next time, OK?' She looked down at the village. 'Still nothing doing, huh?'

Joseph could hear the relief in her voice. He felt it too. He settled back into the grass. Maybe there would be a long wait. With luck, the men wouldn't make a move at all.

'It's nice here,' he said politely to Two. 'The trees are good.'

'They're our trees,' Two said proudly. 'Of my father. We have planted them to provide our fuel, so we do not need soon to go into the park for wood.'

Afra squinted up at a pair of emerald green and bright gold roller birds, who were flaunting their gorgeous colours on the topmost branches.

'Seems a shame to cut them,' she said. 'Those little guys seem really happy up there.'

'It's better to grow trees for cutting than to take old trees,' said Joseph. 'People must have wood for their fires or how will they cook their food? Electricity is too expensive for them.'

Afra was still looking up into the tree. She had

relaxed again, and was enjoying the sparkling of the sunlight through the leaves.

'Why don't they get solar?' she said. 'You know, those panel things.' She looked at them both, suddenly excited. 'Wouldn't that be brilliant? I mean totally amazing? If everyone in Kenya had solar power, they wouldn't have to use wood and the forests would be safe, and the birds and animals would have their habitat.'

Joseph looked at her warily. He knew Afra when she was in the grip of a new idea.

'But solar power's expensive,' he said.

'What? Are you crazy? It's free! I mean, it's just sunlight! Who's going to make you pay for that?'

Joseph clicked his tongue in exasperation.

'Afra, where is your brain? It's not the sunlight that costs money. It's the installation. The panels. The batteries.'

'Oh. Yeah, well.' Afra looked crestfallen. 'OK. I guess you're right. Someone needs to work on it, some scientist or technology buff, to make it cheaper.'

'We have solar power in our schools for our lights.' At last, Two was able to get a word in edgeways. 'That is how we can have classes in the evening now.'

'You do?' Afra beamed at him triumphantly. 'You see?'

'OK, OK.' said Joseph.

'But we are very lucky,' said Two. 'No one else can afford to have such a thing.'

It seemed impossible, all of a sudden, that anything dangerous or out of the way could happen on such a peaceful, ordinary afternoon.

Perhaps we've imagined the whole thing, thought Joseph.

He yawned.

'What's the time?' he asked Afra.

She looked at her watch.

'It's noon.'

Joseph wanted to lie back on the grass and forget everything. It would be nice to stay here, just lazing and chatting for the rest of the day, with nothing else to worry about.

'How long do you think they'll stay in the village, Two?' he said.

Two's eyes had hardly left the cluster of houses below.

'The car is still there,' he said. 'But I cannot see the men. I think perhaps they have gone to the bar. If they do not have relatives here, the bar is the only place where they can go.'

He stretched out on the grass, propping himself up on his one arm so that he could still keep watch.

'What happened to your arm, Two?' asked Joseph. 'How did you lose it?'

Afra frowned at him.

'You don't have to tell us if it's kind of painful for you,' she said quickly.

Two looked quizzically at her and she shook her head at herself and laughed self-consciously.

'Painful? It is not painful to talk about it. It was painful before, when I lost it! I was a little kid only. Five or four years old. I was returning with my father from a village far away, where my uncle lives. We were too late and it had become night. It was a hyena. He ran out of the darkness and took my arm.'

'A hyena? Ate your arm?' Afra was staring at him in horror. 'That's the most scary thing I ever heard in my life!'

Two nodded.

'My father, he was so brave, he beat off the hyena, and he shouted and shouted. People came and ran to us. The hyena ran away. They thought I was going to die, but I didn't. My father – he is the bravest man, even if he is not so healthy now.'

'Wow.' Afra hesitated. 'I guess you can't blame the hyena. That's just how they are.'

Two nodded.

'It is the nature of hyenas,' he said. 'They must snatch for their food.'

Afra looked at him with renewed respect.

'You nearly got killed by a hyena, but you still kind of sympathize with them? And you still creep into a game park full of wild animals? You have real guts.'

Two shrugged.

'I was only a kid then. I can defend myself now.'

'What's that?' Joseph's sensitive ears had picked up a rustling sound nearby. He sat up, his nerves suddenly on edge.

A warthog had trotted up to the far side of the coppice. It was rooting around in the grass with its blunt nose. It looked out, alerted by the sharpened tone in Joseph's voice, and for a moment it stared straight at him.

It looked so comical with its bristly face and little curved tusks, its startled bright eyes and twitching nose, that he had to suppress a crack of laughter.

Then the warthog turned with lightning speed and galloped off, its tight little buttocks bobbing busily across the open ground beyond the trees.

'Did you see him?' began Joseph. 'Wasn't he . . .'

Afra grabbed his arm and shook it.

'Sh!' she hissed.

Joseph looked at her, then turned to see what she was staring at.

Chege and the two men from the car had suddenly emerged from the village and were climbing fast up the hill.

9

POACHERS!

The midday sun was so bright and the shade where they were was so dense that Joseph calculated they must be almost invisible under the trees. He and Two were wearing dark-coloured clothes. Only Afra, in her white T-shirt and blue trousers, would be easy to see. She had obviously come to the same conclusion and was sliding out of sight behind him.

Motionless, his heart pounding, Joseph watched the men come on. He was almost convinced they had spotted them and were coming straight for them, and he was poised to leap up and run, when they turned off the path and started making for the outer fence of the park.

It was then that Joseph saw that the two men with Chege both carried guns, powerful AK47 rifles, slung over their shoulders.

They couldn't shoot us! They wouldn't dare! he told himself, but he wasn't too sure.

Chege was walking along the fence now, looking carefully at the vegetation that grew against it, as Two had done that morning. He dropped to his knees suddenly.

'They're going into the park!' whispered Two excitedly. 'They are poachers!'

'The rhino mother!' gasped Afra, sitting up with a jerk. 'They'll find her and get her!'

The others pushed her down again.

'Watch out!' hissed Joseph. 'Do you want them to see you?'

Chege had removed the dead bushes from the hole under the outer fence now. He turned and scanned the hillside behind him. In the heat of midday, no one stirred in the village. The whole countryside looked deserted.

The men were talking to each other in low voices but they were too far away for Joseph to pick up the words. He watched them as, one by one, they crawled under the outer fence and kicked away the stones holding down the bushes by the inner fence which Two had so carefully arranged only a couple of hours earlier.

'What are we going to do?' Afra whispered urgently. 'The rhinos might still be close by. There's no time!'

Joseph nodded, too preoccupied to speak. He knew what she was feeling, because he felt it too – a terrible dread for the unsuspecting rhino mother, one of the last survivors of her ancient species, who was even now resting somewhere peacefully under the trees in the noonday heat, her little calf beside her.

He was thinking hard.

'We must go after them. Distract them somehow. Wait – no, two of us must go and follow them. Try to warn the rhino off. The third must get help. It's not far back to the service gate. The ranger can get a message to Uncle Titus.'

'The ranger there has no radio. He can do nothing,' Two said. 'It will waste time only. We must go to the main gate.'

'But it's miles away,' objected Afra. The men were through the inner fence now and were rapidly disappearing out of sight among the trees. 'It'll take hours.'

'There's no choice,' said Joseph. 'Afra, you must go. You can run fast and it's too dangerous for you inside.'

Afra's eyes flashed.

'If you think I care about—'

'If you care or you don't care, it doesn't matter.' Joseph's voice was cracking with anxiety. 'We have no time.'

Afra swallowed hard and Joseph could see that she was thinking too.

'If I go for Titus and the rangers, how will I find you again? I don't know my way around in there.'

Joseph frowned.

'That's a good point. We must have a signal. A bird call, maybe. What about a hoopoe?'

'I'd never hear it. I'll be in a Land Rover, don't forget. Joseph, think about it. Two should go for the rangers. He knows the park. He'll know where to lead them.'

Joseph looked at Two, who shook his head doubtfully.

'Look,' said Afra urgently. 'We're wasting time. You can't go in there after them, Two, don't you see? Chege wants to get you already. If he sees you he might make one of those guys loose his gun off at you.'

Reluctantly, Joseph nodded.

'Afra's right, Two. You must go to the main gate. You can run? With your bad leg and your head?'

'I prefer to run with my two legs,' said Two, flashing him a quick grin. Then, bounding down the hill like a bolting goat, he was off.

Joseph looked at Afra. 'Are you ready for this? It could be really dangerous.'

She didn't answer. She was running towards the fence already.

The men hadn't bothered to arrange the bushes over the hole again, and Joseph and Afra were through both fences and back into the park in a moment. They stood still, their backs to the wire mesh, looking about them for signs of the poachers, every sense alert.

Joseph pointed to the ground. There were fresh tracks in the grass. It was easy to see which way the men had gone.

He shut his eyes for a moment. He was terrified,

desperately wishing he could be safely back at home in Nairobi, wondering how he'd been mad enough to follow a gang of armed poachers, who were, he knew, unlikely to stop at anything to get their prey, into a game park teeming with dangerous wild animals.

He felt Afra move off from beside him and opened his eyes. He was committed now. He'd have to see it through. He was glad, after all, that Afra rather than Two was with him. She might have felt a moment of fear back there under the trees but she was one of the bravest people he'd ever known. Once, she'd set off on her own in the middle of the night into the dark countryside to look for a baby baboon, facing countless dangers. She was fiercely loyal, completely trust-worthy.

If only she keeps her temper and doesn't do anything crazy, he thought, setting off after her.

The trees here were quite far apart, but even so it was impossible to see more than twenty or thirty metres ahead. The sunlight filtering through the branches made shifting patterns of light and shade. Afra's white shirt was horribly visible. Joseph wished he'd made her swap hers with Two's much darker one.

'Wait here,' he said, pulling her behind a tree, to give them the chance of scanning the way ahead.

She shook him off.

'We haven't time. We must keep going.'

They were approaching the picnic spot again, the place with the panoramic view where they'd been that morning. They heard the poachers' voices before they saw them, and this time Afra was the first to take cover behind a clump of bushes.

'I tell you, it was here this morning,' Chege was saying in Swahili, his voice raised angrily. 'A female with a good head of horn on her.'

'White rhino or black?' said one of the men.

'Black. I told you. You'd better watch out. Black are much more aggressive. They'll rush at you for nothing.'

'Where is it, then?' The second man pushed his baseball cap up off his forehead. He had taken the rifle down off his shoulder and was fingering the trigger nervously.

'How should I know?' Chege sounded nervous too. 'They rest up in the middle of the day in the shade. Like I said, we should have come early this morning.'

The other man snorted contemptuously.

'You're so foolish, Chege. You want us to come when all the tourists are out looking for game? You want them to take pictures of us too?'

'OK, you two. Take it easy.' The man with the baseball cap put his hands up in a pacifying gesture. 'Come, we must hunt for it. Think of the dollars, my brothers. It's worth a little trouble.' He looked back towards the trees and Joseph and

Afra ducked down quickly. 'Hey! I think we're lucky. Look, there, down the hill, under that big tree. We've got her. Come, slowly now. Follow me!'

Joseph felt a quiver of horror run through Afra. She darted off to the next bush, trying to look down the hill to catch a glimpse of the rhino. Her white T-shirt flashed like a lamp on a dark night.

Joseph had an idea and quickly began unbuttoning his own dark green shirt. He slipped silently up to Afra and put it over her shoulders.

'Put it on,' he whispered. 'It's easy to see you from miles away.'

Afra shot him a smile, then nodded quickly and put the shirt on over her T-shirt.

'Look,' she breathed. 'Down there.'

The female rhino was standing still, her head lowered, as if she was asleep. A small grey protuberance on the far side of her was all that Joseph could see of the calf.

'What are we going to do?' whispered Joseph frantically. 'Look, they're stalking her.'

He felt helpless, and terribly afraid.

Afra had dropped to her knees and was scrabbling round on the bare earth under the bush.

'Stones,' she whispered. 'Quick, help me!'

She came up with a small pebble, stood up and took aim at the rhino. The stone fell short, pinging harmlessly off a tree. Joseph looked back at the men. They were creeping through the grass, their guns poised in front of them, nearer and nearer to the peacefully dozing rhino.

Throwing caution to the wind, he grabbed a second pebble from Afra's hand, stepped out into the open and flung it with all his might. It bounced off the rhino's back. She started, grunted, and began to weave her great head angrily from side to side.

'Go on,' whispered Joseph. 'Get out of there!'

'Joseph! They've seen you! Get down! We've got to run!' hissed Afra, grabbing at his arm.

Joseph looked back. One of the two men was still aiming at the rhino, but the other had swung round.

'It's those kids!' Chege was shouting in Swahili. 'Don't let them get away!'

The second man was taking aim. Afra was bounding away through the trees, and Joseph tore after her, expecting any moment to be felled by a bullet in his back.

He ran wildly, crashing through the bushes, ignoring the thorns and branches that slashed at his naked chest. He'd had nightmares like this, nightmares of being pursued by lions or elephants or demons.

He had lost sight of Afra now. He had forgotten her. His one aim was to escape and survive.

Then a dead branch hidden in the grass tripped him and he fell.

10

CAUGHT!

Desperately, Joseph scrambled to his feet, but it was no good. A hand like a vice closed on his right arm and a powerful elbow locked round his neck.

Joseph lashed out with his left arm, twisting and turning, trying with all his strength to free himself, but the pressure on his windpipe was too great. He knew it was hopeless.

He stopped struggling and stood still.

'You're making a mistake,' he panted, with all the dignity he could muster. 'You won't get away with it.'

He hadn't seen his captor, who was behind him, but now another man came round to face him. It was the man with the baseball cap.

'You're the one who's made a mistake,' he growled in Swahili. 'You're a little spy.'

'I'm just on holiday here,' Joseph began to say, but the man who was holding him roughly jerked his arm.

'Move!' he said. 'I've got a gun. Go on, move!'

Joseph felt something hard and round press between his shoulder blades and his skin shivered all over. Automatically, although his knees suddenly felt so weak he thought they'd give way under him, he began to trot, following the man in front, who was jogging fast through the trees, back towards where they'd seen the rhino.

His mind refused to take in what was happening.

It'll be OK, he thought. Uncle Titus must be on his way. Afra got away anyhow. She'll meet the Land Rover. She'll help them find me.

They came out near the picnic spot. Afra was sitting hunched on the grass, her head on her knees. Chege was standing over her.

Joseph felt a shock of disappointment and a sharper thrill of fear.

They might kill us, he thought incredulously. They really, really might.

One of his captors gave him a rough shove in the back and he fell down beside Afra. She lifted her head and gave him a wobbly smile. Joseph tried to smile back but his face was too rigid with tension.

Chege and the other two men moved away, arguing in low voices. Joseph listened avidly, but he couldn't hear enough to understand anything. He could tell, though, that Chege was trying to persuade the others to do something and that they were resisting. Every now and then, he turned to indicate Joseph and Afra with an angry sweep of the hand, making Joseph shiver uncontrollably.

He wants them to kill us, he thought.

Suddenly the men seemed to come to some agreement. Chege and the one with the cap moved off, stalking cautiously, towards the cover of the bushes into which the rhino had retreated earlier. The third man squatted down in front of Joseph and Afra, his gun held loosely in his hands.

For a wild moment, Joseph thought of rushing him, of grabbing the gun and trying to knock him out with it, but the man seemed to sense this and his hands tightened, his forefinger nervously caressing the trigger.

Joseph looked sideways at Afra. She was as taut as a violin string. She was looking towards the place where Chege and the other man had disappeared. A sudden sharp wind had come up and it was blowing her hair across her face so that he could not read her expression.

She turned suddenly towards him.

'I can smell something,' she whispered. 'Smoke or something.'

He frowned at her. He didn't want to be distracted. Carefully, he cleared his throat, not wanting to startle their guard.

'Listen, my brother,' he said, speaking softly in case the others were still in earshot.

The guard looked into his eyes for the first time. Joseph saw with surprise that he was younger than he had thought, no more than twenty years old, maybe. He was dressed in sharp cheap clothes and his face was tense with nerves. Beads of sweat had sprouted on his forehead and dark trickles ran down the side of his face.

'We're not your enemies,' Joseph went on cautiously. 'We don't want to hurt you.'

'Be quiet,' the guard said, but his voice, which had tried to sound gruff and threatening, squeaked halfway through.

Joseph felt an insect biting his leg and he moved his hand suddenly to swat it away. At once, the young poacher brought the gun up so that it was pointing right at his head.

'It's – it's OK, brother,' said Joseph, trying to control the quiver in his voice. 'It was only an ant.'

His eyes were on the gun. It was being lowered again, down onto the guard's knees.

Joseph bent his head to sideways to indicate Afra.

'This girl,' he said, 'she's not even Kenyan. Her father's a famous American professor. If she gets hurt there will be big trouble for everyone.'

He was hoping that Afra would play up to him, take on the role he was giving her.

The message seemed to have gone home. The young guard shifted his gaze towards Afra, and Joseph could see that he was studying her, looking at her hair and clothes and shoes. Then he spat contemptuously.

'She's not American,' he said. 'She's not even white.'

'Her father's American,' said Joseph, quietly but insistently. 'Her mother was Ethiopian. Look at her skin, brother. She's not dark like us. Her mother's dead. She's her father's only child. He'll make a big scandal and there'll be police everywhere, a huge hunt, for anyone who . . . who hurts her.'

His voice faltered.

The poacher was looking at Afra again. Joseph saw with relief that she had understood and was acting out her part. She had assumed an aloof expression, and was pretending that she couldn't understand Joseph's rapid Swahili. Joseph could see the anxious pucker deepening on the poacher's forehead.

'If you come away with us,' Joseph said, 'we'll tell everyone how you saved us from the other two. Professor Tovey will give you a big reward.'

Afra's head swivelled round at the sound of her father's name.

'What are you telling him?' she demanded haughtily.

'I am telling him that you are an American citizen,' Joseph said, slowly and clearly so that the man would understand. 'He will be in big trouble, bad trouble if anything happens to you.'

Afra nodded.

'Oh boy,' she said with relish, eyeing the guard

defiantly. 'Would he ever. And you tell him that you're practically my brother and Prof will make just as big a stink if they leave a scratch on you, either.'

Joseph felt a glow round his heart for a moment, and his fear lifted a little. He turned back to the guard.

'It's not far to the fence,' he said coaxingly. 'We could be through it very quickly.'

He saw indecision in the man's face as his eyes flickered towards Afra, then back to Joseph again.

He's weakening, he thought, holding his breath.

Then, over the guard's shoulder, he saw Chege and the other man running towards them and the flame of hope went out.

I should have tackled him and got the gun off him, he thought furiously. I've missed our only chance.

Chege was looking angry. He spoke roughly to the young guard who jumped up and backed away. Chege took the gun out of his hands and came up till he was standing right over Joseph and Afra.

He's going to shoot us! thought Joseph wildly. He's really going to do it.

'No! No!' he heard himself babbling. 'Wait! You don't understand!'

Beside him, Afra made a little mewing noise and grabbed his arm. He put his own round her. Then he felt her stiffen.

'Watch out!' she yelled, pointing behind the men.

The three of them whipped round.

The mother rhino had broken out of the cover of the bushes. She was racing towards them, her head lowered, her feet thundering over the ground.

Joseph leaped to his feet and yanked Afra to hers. In an instant the poachers and their guns were wiped from his mind. The instinct to run from an angry animal had taken over them all and he and Afra bolted on winged feet, making for the nearest tree.

He reached it, and darted behind its thick trunk. Afra piled in behind him and they both looked out fearfully. The rhino had veered off to the left and was charging at Chege who was running like a man possessed, his shirt tails flapping out behind him.

Then it seemed to Joseph as if everything slowed down, as if he was watching a film in slow motion. Chege, desperate to escape, flung the gun down onto the grass. The young poacher ran for it and picked it up, raised it to his shoulder and aimed at the rhino. The crash of the report reverberated through the forest. The rhino flinched a little, but without slackening her pace she charged on, and Joseph could see now that her calf was gamely running after her, trying to keep up. Beside him he was aware of Afra's anguished moan of horror, then heard it change to a gasp.

Something new was happening. A crackling, roaring sound was coming from the direction of the picnic spot. He turned to look and saw a sheet of flame advancing at an incredible speed towards him.

The park was on fire.

11

THE MAN WITH THE BASEBALL CAP

Joseph's feeling that he was living through a nightmare returned with full force. He wanted one thing only, to get out of the park and run, leaving the fire and the rhinos and the poachers as far away as possible.

'We've got to get out!' he shouted to Afra. 'Come on!'

He took a few running paces and then stopped. Which way was the fence? They'd run so fast away from the rhino, that he'd lost his sense of direction.

Afra was already racing away from the fire. She looked over her shoulder at him.

'What are you waiting for?' she yelled. 'You want to get roasted alive?'

Joseph took off after her. He seemed to have lost the power to make decisions, as if he was watching himself from far away.

He heard something crashing through the undergrowth behind him and flinched, afraid that Chege and the poachers might be after them again, but it was only a couple of bushbuck who were fleeing with wide eyes and distended nostrils from the flames.

Ahead of him he saw Afra pull up short. He caught her up.

'Look!' she panted, pointing in front of her. 'We're going right towards the cliff! We'll be cut off!'

She was right. He could see through the trees that the ground dropped suddenly away, and below, in the distance, an unreal vision of peace and beauty, was the tranquil lake.

'Come this way,' he said, pulling at her sleeve and setting off again at an oblique angle to the fire. 'We'll try to get round to the side of it.'

They sprinted off again.

They both heard the snorting, bellowing sound at the same time. The rhino was galloping away from the fire in a straight line directly towards the edge of the cliff. The calf was nowhere to be seen.

'No!' Afra shrieked after her. 'Look out!'

The rhino veered a little to one side and a billow of smoke hid her from view.

'She's so blind she won't see the cliff till she's right on top of it!' cried Afra. 'She'll go right over!'

'We can't help her now,' said Joseph. 'Come on!'

They raced on, leaping over fallen branches

and dodging between the bushes that slashed at Joseph's naked chest.

They slowed down at last, out of breath, and looked back. The wind appeared to have changed. The fire was no longer following them. It was blowing back on itself. It had rapidly covered the last few metres to the cliff top where Joseph and Afra had been a few minutes earlier, but it was not advancing any further along the top of the cliff towards them.

Something else was advancing though. The older poacher with the baseball cap was hopping towards them, limping as if he'd hurt his leg. His rifle was slung over his shoulder on the strap and he had one hand up to his face as if he'd bruised it.

'He hasn't seen us,' whispered Joseph. 'Quick! Hide!'

He pulled Afra behind a thick stand of bushes. He suddenly knew what he had to do next and it seemed ridiculously easy.

The man was coming in their direction making for the very bush where they were hiding, as Joseph had somehow known he would. Joseph bent down and picked up a long stick lying conveniently on the ground, then, crouching down, he thrust it out at knee level just as the man was passing.

With a surprised grunt, the poacher tripped and fell on his face. In an instant, Joseph was on top of him, pinning him to the ground.

'Take the gun!' Joseph yelled to Afra who, too surprised to move, was still standing behind the bush, her mouth agape.

She came to her senses with a jerk, leapt forward, grabbed the gun and brandished it triumphantly in the air.

'Joseph! You genius! We've got him!'

The man was struggling violently, but although he was big and powerful, Joseph could tell by his grunts of pain that his wounded leg was hurting him.

'Afra, stop!' he commanded. 'Take off my shirt and give it to me. Quickly!'

Afra calmed down immediately and ripped off the shirt.

'Hold his arms,' said Joseph. 'Hurry!'

He was panting with the effort. The man was like a bucking horse, writhing and twisting, trying to shake Joseph off. Holding one sleeve of his shirt in his teeth, Joseph managed to make a noose.

'Hold his wrists,' he said. 'Yes, that's it.'

He slipped the noose round one of the man's wrists and pulled it tight, managing with difficulty to get it over the other. Then he wrenched the two bound wrists together and tied them securely.

'He can still run,' said Afra. 'You'd better tie his legs.'

'He won't run,' said Joseph in Swahili, sounding as threatening as he could. 'He knows we have the gun and we'll shoot him at once if he tries to run away.'

He felt the fight go out of the man and cautiously released his grip. The man lay still, obviously frightened. Gingerly, Joseph picked up the gun. He'd never held one before and he was scared that it would go off. He poked the man with his foot.

'Get up,' he growled, trying to sound fierce.

The poacher rose slowly to his knees and tried to look up but Afra leaned forward and pulled the peak of his cap right down so that it was almost obscuring his eyes.

'That'll slow you down, baby,' she said with satisfaction. Then she turned to Joseph. 'What do we do now, boss?'

She'd never called him that before. She usually elbowed her way into the lead. Joseph was on his mettle. He thought quickly.

'We walk him out through the fence and down to the village,' he said decisively.

'What if we meet Chege and the other one?' objected Afra.

'We must go slowly and watch out for them,' said Joseph. 'It's better if you go on ahead. I'll go behind with this guy and the gun.'

'Hey, do you think he speaks English?' Afra had lowered her voice to a whisper.

'A bit, maybe,' said Joseph. 'But I think he is stupid and ignorant. Let's see.'

He lifted the peak of the baseball cap for a moment and said, right into the man's face, 'A spider is crawling up your right arm. It's going inside your shirt and it's going to bite you. It will inject you with deadly poison.'

The man stared back at him impassively and his arm didn't even twitch.

'He can't speak English,' said Joseph, pulling the peak down again. 'Not much, anyway.'

He turned the man round and bent down surreptitiously to pick up a stick. He couldn't bear to point the gun at him. He prodded the man with the stick, hoping he would think it was the gun, and took hold of the loose sleeve of his shirt which was dangling from the man's bound wrists.

'Move,' he said curtly.

Afra had already started off, scouting out the way ahead. It would be easy to find the fence now that they knew where the cliff was. They had only to walk directly away from it. The fire was still burning fiercely, but it had stopped advancing, and the wind was blowing the choking clouds of smoke away from them, over the edge of the cliff.

The poacher stumbled forward. His leg was clearly hurting him and he was limping badly. Joseph resisted the temptation of asking him what had happened to it although the man seemed so dejected that Joseph almost felt sorry for him. It was a bad idea, though, to get too friendly with your prisoner. They could take advantage of you more easily. He'd learned that with the other poacher.

Ahead of him, Afra had stopped. She turned round and signalled to him to wait. Then he saw her duck behind a tree. A moment later he heard the sound that must have startled her. It was the noise of a Land Rover engine.

He yanked on the shirt sleeve and the man stopped moving.

It's got to be Uncle Titus and the rangers! Joseph thought. Or a fire-fighting team.

But he felt wary, afraid in case for some reason the poachers had friends, a back-up vehicle that could even now be approaching.

The Land Rover appeared between the trees. Joseph heard Afra cry out, 'It's all right! It's the Kenya Wildlife Service,' and saw her dash out to flag it down.

The Land Rover skidded to a halt and Omondi leaned out of the window. Joseph could see that the Land Rover was packed with men in rangers' uniforms, but only one caught his attention. The man in the back seat, nearest the window, was Chege.

Chege opened the door and jumped out.

'There!' he said in a blustering voice to Omondi, who was climbing out of the Land Rover too. 'What did I tell you? Poachers! And these kids are in league with them.'

He was speaking Swahili, and Joseph heard his

prisoner draw in his breath with sharp indignation and saw him lift his head, trying to peer out from under the low peak.

'Poachers? Us?' Joseph's voice almost squeaked with fury and he did his best to lower it. 'This guy's a poacher. He's been hunting the female black rhino.' He pointed his stick at his drooping prisoner. 'And you are one of them!' He waved the stick at Chege. 'If I'm a poacher, why have I tied this man up? Ask him. Go on. Ask Chege.'

Chege was backing away from the Land Rover, spreading his hands out placatingly.

'What is this nonsense? You know me, my friends. I am Chege, your old colleague. How can I be doing criminal activities with these kinds of people? I used to work with you. The kid's lying. He's nothing but a troublemaker. Who is he, anyway? He's not from around here.'

Joseph looked desperately at Omondi.

'Don't you remember me, Mr Omondi? We were with you when you darted Wildfire.'

Omondi had been studying Joseph, as if he was trying to remember him, but now a smile broke out on his broad face, creasing his plump cheeks.

'It's Joseph! Of course I remember you!'

He looked back at Chege, his eyes narrowing.

'You see? He knows me! He knows I'm Titus Musau's nephew!' Joseph shouted furiously to Chege.

The men had been wavering, not sure what to

do, but at the mention of Titus's name they all looked round and stared at Chege. Chege's eyes went rapidly from one to the other, then he turned and began to bolt off through the trees.

'Stop him!' yelled Afra and Joseph together. 'Don't let him get away!'

Two of the rangers took off after Chege, and a moment later had caught up with him. They grappled with him for a moment, but Chege, a big, powerful man, fought with the added strength of desperation. He punched one of the rangers to the ground, then bent down and in one swift movement seized his gun. The other leaped on him, but Chege, with violent force, shook him off and darted away through the trees.

Joseph had almost forgotten his own prisoner, but suddenly he felt a tug on the sleeve he was holding as the man also made a sudden bid for freedom. Just in time, Joseph tightened his grip.

'Stop that!' he said, as gruffly as he could. 'Do you want a bullet in your ribs?' and he poked his stick into the man's back to make his threat sound more realistic.

There were confused shouts ahead and he looked up again. Another Land Rover had appeared, and a familiar figure was climbing out of the front seat. Joseph felt a sob of pure relief well up in his throat.

'Uncle Titus!' he yelled. 'Oh, thank God! You've come!'

12

THE FOOTBALL TEAM TO THE RESCUE

Men spilled out of the second Land Rover. They ran off towards the fire and began pounding on the smouldering grass.

Joseph stiffened a little as Titus ran towards him. He and Afra had broken the cardinal rule of the game park and had entered it alone and on foot.

After all this, after all *this*, if he's angry with me I won't take it, he thought.

But Titus looked bewildered rather than angry. His eyes took in Joseph's bare chest, his torn and dirt-smeared trousers, the rifle slung over his shoulder, and the man cowering in front of him, whose arms were still bound behind his back, and who was still blinded by the baseball cap over his eyes.

'Joseph, what happened? Who is this man? Who started the fire?'

Joseph felt suddenly weak. He wanted to sit down on the grass and cry. He knew he was trembling from head to foot and tried in vain to stop. Beside him, Afra had slumped down onto a fallen branch. Her shoulders were heaving and her face was buried in her hands.

'He's one of the poachers,' Joseph said. 'We caught him. We thought they were going to kill us. Especially Chege. He's the leader. He got away, just now. He ran off over there.' He pointed through the trees. 'They nearly did kill us. They were about to . . . to shoot us.' He felt sick suddenly, and stopped.

Afra looked up.

'The rhino saved us,' she said, 'just in time. And then she – I think she ran over the cliff and the baby wasn't even with her.'

Her face crumpled again.

Omondi drew in his breath sharply.

'The female rhino?' he said. 'She went over the edge?'

He started hastily towards the cliff. Titus called him back.

'Leave her till later,' he said. 'We must deal with these criminals and the fire first.'

He turned and called to one of the rangers who was still unloading fire-fighting equipment.

'Come and take this prisoner. Get him into handcuffs and don't let him get away.'

He unhitched the rifle from Joseph's shoulder and prised Joseph's fingers off the sleeve of the shirt, which he was still compulsively clutching.

One of the rangers hoisted the poacher to his feet and put him in a strong armlock while

Omondi untied Joseph's shirt and snapped hand-cuffs round the man's wrists. Then with an admiring smile he handed the shirt back to Joseph.

'I've known rhinos like you,' he said. 'Strong and daring.'

Joseph took the shirt without answering. He didn't know what to say.

Titus laughed.

'Coming from Omondi, that's a great compliment,' he called over to him.

Joseph began to put the shirt on, but the acrid, sour smell of the prisoner's sweat rose from it. It made him feel sick again. He let it dangle from his hand.

There was a shout from the firefighters.

'Stay here,' said Titus, sprinting off towards them.

Joseph sank down onto the branch beside Afra.

'I feel so weird,' she said. 'Kind of weepy and weak.'

He felt relieved.

'I do too.'

'I guess we're in shock.' She laughed shakily. 'Who wouldn't be, after nearly being shot by poachers, and charged by a rhino, and almost getting caught in a bush fire?'

He laughed too. He felt a bit stronger now. He put his shirt on. He couldn't smell the poacher any more. He felt better with it on. More normal.

'Where's Two?' he said.

Afra's head jerked up and she looked round.

'Two! I actually forgot all about him.'

'Maybe Uncle Titus told him to go home. Maybe he thought it was too dangerous for him to come back.'

'But Two was going to show him where we were, remember?'

Titus was coming back towards them. He looked worried.

'There's bad news, I'm afraid. The men have found the tracks of the female black rhino. She was running fast towards the cliff.'

'I knew it! I saw her! Oh, it's so horrible!' Afra banged a fist down onto her knees. 'I called out to her and she kind of ran sideways a little but I guess it wasn't enough.'

'The tracks don't go right up to the edge,' said Titus, 'because the ground's hard and rocky there. There's still a little hope. I've sent a radio message to the headquarters for a team to go and search for her below the cliff.'

'What about the calf?' said Afra. 'Where is he?'

'There are no tracks from the calf,' said Titus. 'As soon as the fire's out, we'll start to search for him, but we have no one to spare at the moment. All the men are needed to put out the fire.'

Omondi shook his head. He did it slowly and despondently, and, for a moment, he reminded Joseph of a rhino.

'If she fell over the cliff,' he said, 'there is no hope for her. It will soon be getting dark. We cannot look for her until the morning.'

'It's just so cruel,' said Afra. 'After she escaped from three murdering poachers, to die in a stupid accident.'

'Three! Of course, there was the other one!' Joseph jumped up. 'Uncle Titus, there were three of them. The third one ran away. And he still has a gun!'

'What?' Titus's brows snapped together. 'Which way did he go?'

'I didn't see. We were running away from the fire,' said Joseph.

'He'll have run back to the fence,' said Afra. 'He'll have escaped out of the park by now.'

Titus shook his head.

'He can't get over the fence. It's electrified.'

Joseph and Afra looked at each other guiltily.

'There's a place where there's a kind of hole under the fence,' said Joseph bravely. 'Two showed it to us. That's how we came in ourselves.'

Titus rolled up his eyes.

'Joseph, you'll make me die of fright one day if you don't kill yourself first. Come on, quickly. Show me where this place is.'

'I'm not sure if we can,' said Afra. 'Where's Two? He's the one who really knows the way.'

'Two?' said Titus.

'The boy with one arm. We called him Two. Where is he?'

'Oh, yes. He's a first class runner, that kid,' said Titus. 'He came into headquarters at the main gate so fast, I thought a leopard was chasing him. I was worried about him because he had a bad bruise on his face and a bandage on his leg, but he told us it was OK, it didn't hurt him any more. We brought him with us in the Land Rover to the service gate, but he was feeling sick. He said he wasn't used to travelling in cars. He pointed out the direction to us and we let him out.'

Afra and Joseph exchanged looks.

'But it's hardly any distance from the main gate,' objected Afra. 'It certainly can't be enough to set off motion sickness.'

'It doesn't matter now,' Uncle Titus said. 'We must go after the third poacher. Come on, let's go!'

He began to run back to the nearest Land Rover, calling as he went to Omondi, who had run off to help the firefighters. They were working more slowly now. The fire had almost burned itself out. A few bushes were still ablaze, and the grass was smouldering, but the worst was over. It had been a quick brush fire and hadn't had time to take a serious hold.

Joseph and Afra jumped into the front of the Land Rover and the men climbed into the back. Titus began to drive over the rough ground.

'What does he look like, this poacher?' he said.

'Slim. Young,' said Joseph. 'He's not at all educated. He can hardly speak any English. He's wearing a black and grey striped shirt and khaki trousers. His trainers are black and grey.'

'Well done.' Titus looked down at him approvingly. 'You're a good witness. You observed him carefully.'

'We had plenty of time to look at him,' said Joseph, shuddering at the memory. 'He was standing over us with a gun.'

Titus was driving so fast that a few moments later they were at the service gate. The ranger was hovering beside it, keyed up by the unusual comings and goings. He came up to Titus's window and saluted smartly.

'Have you seen anyone come through here?' said Titus. 'A man with a black and grey shirt? He has a gun.'

The ranger shook his head slowly.

'I must think,' he said, relishing his moment in the limelight. 'Earlier this morning there was a truck. It had supplies in it for the tourist lodge. Then the workmen came through, those ones from the village who are laying down the new road. After that—'

'But you haven't seen a man alone on foot, with a gun?' Titus broke impatiently into the ranger's flow.

'No sir,' the ranger said regretfully. 'But there

was a man with a boy. It was that one-armed boy, Isaac, from the village. And the man was holding him tight, you know, by the collar. They were running past here, down the hill. "This boy has been caught in some mischief," I thought. "Probably he is being punished." '

'But did the man have a gun?' interrupted Titus.

The ranger put his head on one side as if to help him think more clearly.

'A gun? I did not see him clearly, sir. Maybe there was something in his hand. A stick, I thought, but perhaps – a gun? I don't—'

'Which way were they going?' said Titus curtly.

'Down there, sir.' The ranger, responding at last to Titus's impatience, pointed decisively towards the village.

Titus slammed the Land Rover into gear and set off down the bumpy track at a furious pace.

'It sounds as if the poacher has captured Two!' Joseph said anxiously. 'Do you think he's taken him hostage?'

Titus looked grim.

'Yes, Joseph. That's exactly what I think. We must find him at once!'

They were on the outskirts of the village now. As if from nowhere, a crowd of boys had appeared. They raced towards the Land Rover, trying to flag it down.

'Get away from the car!' Titus shouted impatiently. 'What's the matter with these kids?

They have nothing better to do with themselves, just running after every car that comes through their village!'

Joseph looked back at the boys as the car sped on.

'I think they want to talk to you, Uncle Titus,' he said doubtfully.

'I'm sure they want to talk to me,' Titus said, negotiating a sudden dip in the track with as much speed as he safely could. 'I visit the school here every time I come. Last time they made me play football. I couldn't move for a whole week afterwards.'

'Look!' Joseph and Afra shouted together. 'There they are!'

They had turned the corner and were coming down towards the empty space at the edge of the village where the football game had taken place. The white car was still parked at the edge of it, and walking towards it, with a stalking motion like a cat, was the young poacher. In front of him, the gun in his back, walked Two.

The poacher turned his head at the sound of the Land Rover coming down into the village behind him, grabbed hold of Two's arm and pulled him round in front of him to shield himself.

'Take it easy,' muttered Titus under his breath. 'Just take it easy.'

He brought the Land Rover gently to a halt

and switched off the engine. Then he leaned out of the window.

'Let the boy go,' he said, in a calm, authoritative voice.

Even from this distance Joseph could see the panic in the poacher's eyes. He didn't answer, but stood indecisively, his eyes darting from side to side. Joseph looked round too. The village seemed deserted. People had clearly scattered at the approach of the man with the gun. Joseph could see a few heads cautiously peering out from between the houses. Then a movement beside the Land Rover caught his eye. The boys who had been chasing them earlier had caught up with them. He recognized them now. They were the boys from the football team.

Their arrival seemed to alarm the poacher and he waved his gun wildly at them.

'Get back!' he shouted. 'Leave me alone, or I'll kill him!'

He jerked Two's arm violently, nearly making him lose his balance, then he began backing towards the car.

'Stop him!' breathed Afra. 'We've got to stop him!'

Titus cautiously opened the door of the Land Rover and slid out. He took a couple of steps towards the poacher.

'No!' the man screamed, and his voice sounded hysterical. 'Don't come any nearer! I'll shoot!'

Titus took another step forward, but then, from behind, four of the boys took a flying leap at him and tackled him to the ground.

'What – what? Stop it! Get off!' Titus bellowed furiously, then stopped abruptly as one of the boys clamped a hand over his mouth.

Still in the Land Rover, Joseph had watched in stunned amazement, but before he had a chance to think out what to do, everything happened at once.

The poacher, startled by the brawl over Titus, made a dash for his car, hauling Two after him. He bundled him into the front and launched himself into the driver's seat.

'No!' shrieked Afra, halfway out of the Land Rover already. 'Let him go!'

Joseph clutched at her T-shirt and pulled her back inside.

'Do you want him to shoot Two?' he said. 'He'll do it if he panics completely.'

He was waiting with dread for the sound of the car's engine to roar into life, and for the car to race off down the track away from the village with Two a prisoner inside it. He could see the driver hunched over the wheel, turning and turning the key in the ignition, but no sound came.

Then suddenly, two small figures inside the car leapt up from the back seat and four arms were hanging on to the poacher's neck and arms. It was impossible to see now what was going on, as the car was filled with a confusion of heads and arms.

'What's happening?' gasped Afra. 'Where's Two? Who are those kids in the car?'

The passenger door of the car burst open and Two staggered out of it, holding the gun in his hand. At once, the four boys who had been holding Titus down jumped up.

'We are very sorry, sir,' one of them said, grinning at him triumphantly. 'We didn't have time to explain to you our plan. We were afraid you would spoil everything! You can take him now, the poacher. We have caught him for you.'

For a moment, Titus glared at them.

'You young criminals,' he said. 'Have you no respect?' Then his face broke into an appreciative grin. 'I'll think of your punishment later.' And he began to run across the empty ground towards the white car.

Afra and Joseph tumbled out of the Land Rover into the crowd of jubilant boys, and together they raced after Titus. He had reached the car already and was hauling the bedraggled young poacher out of it.

'We caught him! We ambushed him!' The boys had formed a ring around the car and were performing victorious leaps, clapping and chanting like warriors after a famous battle.

Two came up to Joseph and Afra.

'Are you all right? What happened in there?' He jerked his head towards the park. 'Did they catch Chege?'

'No. He ran off, but we caught the other one,' said Joseph, who was looking bewildered. 'They captured us first, and then the rhino charged at them, and then there was a fire, and we think the rhino went over the cliff. It's too much to explain. But what happened to you? Why did those boys jump on Uncle Titus? Who were the ones in the car?'

Two punched the air jubilantly.

'You called me Two-brains,' he said proudly, 'and you were right. I was very clever. I was afraid that the men could easily escape from the park. I came back with your uncle to the service gate and I told them I felt sick.'

'You mean you didn't feel sick?' Afra nodded at Joseph. 'We didn't think so.'

'I did, a bit, and my head was aching very much, but really it was an excuse,' said Two. 'Before, when I was running to the gate to find your uncle, I had met some of the boys and I had told them everything. I told Eliezer to make the car so that it would not go.'

'That was brilliant!' said Afra admiringly. 'How did he do that?'

'It was easy for him.' Two shrugged. 'His father, he owns a *matatu* bus. He has taught Eliezer about engines.'

'Then what?' demanded Afra.

'I told some of the boys: Wait up by the fence and see what will happen. And to the others I said: Wait beside the car and we will see if we can capture the men on our own.'

'You don't mean,' said Afra, awestruck, that you deliberately got that man to take you hostage?'

'No!' Two shuddered. 'That was the worst part. I made a mistake. After your uncle put me down from the Land Rover I went along the fence on the outside towards the hole. I wanted to ask my friends who were waiting near there: Have you seen anyone? My friends were hiding in the trees where we waited earlier. Before I could reach them, this criminal, he crawled out through the hole in the fence and caught hold of my foot, like this.'

He put his hand down to make an awkward grab at his ankle. 'I was so frightened.'

'I know.' Joseph nodded. 'He caught us too. We were really terrified. What did your friends do when they saw he'd caught you?'

'What can they do? This poacher, he has a gun in my back. If they disturb him, they know he will certainly shoot me. Out of the corner of my eyes, I can see one of my friends running around behind, down towards the village. I know he is warning the others that the poacher is coming. But the other boys, I do not know. They made a plan, I think, to stop your uncle and tell him what is happening.'

Joseph nodded.

'We know that part, but who were the boys in the car?'

Two beamed.

'They are Daniel and Caleb. They are centre forwards – our best strikers! That was the best part. They saw there is only one poacher coming so they climbed quietly into the back of the car ready to overpower him.'

'But wasn't the car locked?' said Afra.

'Locked? Yes, of course it was locked!' Two laughed. 'But what is a car lock to Eliezer?'

'Look, here they come,' said Afra suddenly, pulling Joseph aside.

He looked round. Titus was frogmarching the young poacher towards the Land Rover. The crowd of boys was following. Joseph, Afra and Two fell in with them.

'Look in the front locker of the Land Rover, Joseph,' said Titus. 'There are handcuffs there. Bring them out to me.'

Joseph opened the door of the Land Rover, found the handcuffs and passed them to Titus. They closed on the man's wrists with a satisfying click that brought another cheer from the victorious crowd of boys.

The poacher looked into Joseph's eyes, then looked sideways at Two.

'I did not want to kill you,' he said, with an ingratiating smile. 'I am a poor man. My family is poor.'

The boys all fell silent.

'Get in,' said Titus, pushing the poacher into the back of the Land Rover. He took the gun off Two's shoulder, where he had been triumphantly carrying it, and laid it carefully below the front seat. Then he looked at Two.

'Are you all right, son?' he said.

Two shook his head. He was suddenly looking dazed.

'I think ... I feel ...' he began, and then sat down and put his head on his knees.

Several of the boys clucked sympathetically, and crouched down beside him.

'Take him home,' Titus said. 'Tell his mother to make him rest. This boy runs like a cheetah and thinks like a fox, but even cheetahs and foxes have to rest.'

He climbed back into the driving seat.

'Guard the prisoner, you kids,' he said over his shoulder to Joseph and Afra, who were in the back seat, one on each side of the poacher. 'After everything else you've done today, you won't find that very difficult!'

13

CHEGE ON THE RUN

No one talked in the Land Rover as Titus drove away from the village. The boys ran after it for a while, still chanting triumphantly, but once they'd been left behind, a tense silence descended. The presence of the young poacher sitting between Joseph and Afra in a sweat of nervous misery was a strain.

Joseph felt completely exhausted and dazed too. He stared out of the window at the landscape bumping past. It felt like being in a cage with a wild animal who had tried to leap at his throat and worry him, but was now muzzled and chained. Given the slightest chance, he knew, the man would make a break and run for it. Joseph felt a strange mixture of fear, disgust and pity.

He couldn't get out of his mind the moment when he'd looked up into Chege's cold eyes and seen murder in them. Something had happened inside him, and he felt he'd never be the same again. It was as if he really had died at that moment, and that now he'd started being alive all over again but in a different way.

The things which had seemed important before

didn't seemed to matter any more. He didn't feel scared now in case Uncle Titus was angry with him. He thought fleetingly of his exam. Even that felt different. He'd work for it, and he'd either pass it or he wouldn't. Whatever happened, he'd still be all right. Everything from now on would be all right. He felt confident as he'd never felt before.

For some reason, his father's face came into his mind.

I wish he could see me now, he thought. I wish he knew what I'd done. He'd be proud of me, I know he would.

Titus braked suddenly, and the Land Rover skidded to a halt. Joseph had been looking unseeingly out to one side, but now he looked ahead. A police car was coming up the track. Titus leaned out of his window as the car pulled up alongside.

'Good,' he said to the two policemen in the car. 'Headquarters got through to you at last. There's one man still on the loose. He knows the park well – used to be a ranger here – and he's armed, so he will be dangerous. But he's alone and on foot. He can't be very far away.' He jerked his head towards the back seat. 'We've caught one of the other two fellows for you. He was in the act of hunting a rhino.' His shoulders heaved as he laughed. 'You guys had better watch out. You have some very stiff competition in this village from the kids.'

He jumped out and opened the back door of the Land Rover.

'Get out,' he said shortly to the poacher.

Afra climbed out first and the poacher stumbled awkwardly after her. He turned for one last look at Joseph. The pity Joseph had started to feel for him died abruptly. The man had stopped trying to arouse a sense of fellow feeling in his captors, and in his eyes there was only pure malevolence.

'You dirty little . . .' he began to spit out, but the two policemen took hold of his arms and manhandled him into the back of the police car.

Titus looked at Joseph, who was still sitting in the back seat.

'Come into the front with me,' he said, opening the front passenger door invitingly.

Joseph hopped into the front and Afra climbed in beside him. Now that the poacher had gone, everything seemed different. Joseph's mood changed. He was euphoric, filled with a bubble of pure joy.

'I ought to give you a bad time,' Titus said, looking sideways at him.

Joseph smiled back at him. Uncle Titus looked horribly stern when he was angry. He didn't look at all stern now.

Titus shook his head, wonderingly.

'Those kids! Jumping on me like that! And putting an ambush in the car! I couldn't believe my own eyes.'

'That was all Two's idea,' said Joseph happily. 'He's brilliant. We call him Two, short for Two-brains, because it's a better name than One-arm, and he deserves it. He has three brains!'

Titus let out the brake and began to drive on.

'But what happened? Where does this boy come into it? And how did you discover the poachers?'

'It was last night.' Joseph wriggled in his seat and settled into his story. 'We heard someone shouting, and we ran and found Chege beating Two. Two told us Chege used to work in the park, but he was fired. Two had just seen him, taking money from the gate, and Chege looked up and saw him watching.'

Titus's brows briefly snapped together.

'You should have told me this at once,' he said.

'Two made us promise. He said Chege would kill him. He didn't have any proof that Chege was a thief. Maybe no one would believe his story, he said.'

Titus nodded.

'That's understandable. But what I want to know is this. Why did you go into the park? And on foot? You know it's absolutely against the rules?'

Joseph took a deep breath. He was nervous about this part of his story.

'Two took us in to . . . to see the rhino and her calf. It would be safe, that's what he thought, because her range is always down below the cliff and near to the lake. She never comes where we were, so close to the viewing place where the tourists walk around. We were going to look down on her just from above.'

'Your friend may be very clever,' Titus said drily, 'but he's lacking in common sense. Rhinos are creatures of habit, but they're not that predictable. And then?'

'We saw the rhino, very close, with the calf, and it was so ... I felt proud to be me, Uncle Titus, to be an African. I felt she was somehow ... I can't explain it clearly. It was like I had known her for many, many years. Before I was born, even.'

Titus looked at him.

'You feel that too, do you?'

'Yes.'

Joseph said nothing for a moment, waiting for the storm to break, but Titus was turning in through the main gate of the park and said nothing.

'Tell me the rest later,' he said. He looked beyond him at Afra.

'You're very quiet,' he said.

Afra shook her head.

'I'm so ashamed of myself,' she mumbled.

'What?' Joseph hadn't heard her clearly.

'I said this morning I'd lay down my life for that rhino,' Afra said, a bit louder. 'But when that creep was about to do it, to kill us, I mean, I'd have sacrificed anything, anyone, just to stay alive. I guess I didn't know myself too well. And now I can't bear to think of her, the rhino, and her calf, especially the calf, lost somewhere and scared to death and all on their own. I keep thinking we could have done more, been a little more clever or something maybe, and at least saved one of them.'

Her voice trailed away.

Titus had pulled up outside the warden's house.

'It's a little too early to be so upset, Afra,' he said. 'We don't know anything for sure. I'm going back now to make sure the fire is fully dealt with. The most important thing we can do tonight is to see that no sparks are left which can start burning again. Omondi's going to lead the search tomorrow morning. He knows all the rhinos in the park, just as if they were people. He'll know where to look. Don't worry. We'll search behind every bush and under every tree. If – *if* the female rhino is dead and the calf's alive, he'll go to the animal orphanage. He'll be well looked after there.'

'But Chege's still out there somewhere,' said Joseph, with a shudder. 'Perhaps he'll try to get her again.'

Titus shook his head.

'Chege has the police force of Nakuru and half the park rangers on his trail now. He's thinking about saving his own skin.'

'Do you think they'll catch him?' said Joseph, trying not to sound worried.

'Of course they will. It depends if he managed to get out of the park. They closed the hole as soon as they could, and they're looking out for him carefully at all of the gates, but he might have slipped through. If he's outside, it won't be so easy, but if he's still in the park, we'll get him. Don't worry.'

Afra hadn't been listening.

'I just can't get over how she saved us. She saved our lives.' Her voice was shaking. 'She charged at those . . . those fiends just when they were about to shoot us.'

Titus looked at his watch, then up at the sky.

'I must go back,' he said. 'It'll be getting dark soon. You two, stay here, eat something, drink plenty of water, take a bath and rest.'

Joseph suddenly realized that he was ravenous and extremely thirsty. He nodded gratefully.

'If you like, you can come out in the morning, to help in the search for the female and the calf,' Titus went on. 'OK?'

Joseph nodded.

'Try keeping us away,' said Afra. She opened the door of the Land Rover and she and Joseph stumbled out onto the grass. They stood for a moment, watching the Land Rover disappear back down the track towards the main gate in a cloud of dust. Then from the *boma* a few hundred metres away came a low bellowing and the thwack of a powerful horn on wood.

'It sounds like Wildfire. Maybe he's upset,' said Afra.

'I'm not surprised if he is,' said Joseph. 'You can smell the smoke even down here, far away from the fire. It might be frightening for him. Maybe we should go and check on him.'

Afra was halfway to the house.

'He'll be OK,' she said. 'That *boma*'s strong enough to hold a herd of elephants. Anyway, I'm so thirsty I could drink the entire lake, and then all I want to do is sleep.'

Joseph suddenly realized that he was tired too, exhausted in fact, right down to his bones. He was thirsty as well, more than he had ever been in his life.

He followed Afra into the house, and good smells, wafting down the corridor from the kitchen, filled his nostrils. Automatically, he followed Afra, who was pushing open the door of the kitchen.

Nathan, the cook, was busy frying onions. He turned to glance at them, frowned, and shook his ladle at them.

'Who let you in here?' he said, frowning ferociously.

'Please, Nathan,' said Joseph. 'We won't get in your way. We only want some water.'

The cook looked at them again and his face cleared.

'You are really Joseph and Afra?' he said. 'I was thinking I had never seen these two strange people before. *Aiee!* You are so dirty! And what has happened to your nice clean clothes?'

'It's too long to explain,' said Afra, going to the fridge and pulling out a jug of filtered water.

She poured out two glasses and she and Joseph stood and drank so greedily that water poured down their chins.

'More,' gasped Joseph at last, handing his glass to her for a refill.

'No, no, go slowly,' said Nathan, taking the jug out of Afra's hand. 'Too much cold water all at once will make you sick. Go and wash now. You're too dirty for my kitchen.'

'When's supper going to be ready?' said Afra pleadingly.

'Soon, soon,' said Nathan, shooing them away.

Afra and Joseph sank down into two of the old battered armchairs in the roomy sitting room.

'I can't believe it all happened,' began Joseph. 'That moment when Chege looked at us . . .' He stopped and shuddered. 'He was going to kill us. I mean, he really was going to do it.'

'Mmm,' said Afra, slumping further down against the cushions.

'And Two and Eliezer and all the football team, they were so clever,' Joseph went on.

There was silence from Afra. He looked across at her. She was already fast asleep. Joseph yawned. It was stupid, going to sleep at six o'clock in the evening, when it wasn't even dark yet and they hadn't had supper.

Supper will be ready soon, he thought, and Uncle Titus will be back. Oh I hope, I hope, they find the mother rhino! And the baby.

He remembered how the rhinos had been peacefully feeding that morning, and he saw in his mind's eye the baby's flickering tail and the mother's gently lowered head. Somehow it was easier to think of them with his eyes closed.

In a moment, he was asleep too.

An hour later, there was a confused babble of sound and he half woke. Still dazed, he saw in a fuzz of light Uncle Titus and with him a small, round man with a bald head and a thick moustache, who looked, to Joseph's dazzled eyes, oddly familiar.

'Joseph, Afra,' Titus said. 'Wake up! Look, Dr Ibrahim's here.'

Joseph smiled shakily and tried to struggle to his feet. He was still half asleep. He felt Dr Ibrahim's hand pressing him back down in his chair.

'No, no, you can rest,' Dr Ibrahim said. He had been frowning, but a smile briefly lit his sombre face. 'You kids are the heroes of the day, after all. Give them some food, Titus, and send them to bed.'

'Food, bed,' repeated Joseph, sleepily.

At that moment, they were the most beautiful words in the world.

14

THE RHINO HUNT

Joseph slept all night without stirring. Titus woke him when it was still almost dark by gently shaking his foot. Joseph sat bolt upright at once, his eyes wide and staring.

'No!' he said thickly. 'Don't shoot!'

For an awful moment he had thought that the big dark shape at the foot of his bed was Chege.

Titus was already halfway out of the door.

'It's nearly dawn,' he said. 'Get up if you want to come with us. We're going out to look for the rhinos.'

He went off to wake Afra.

Joseph jumped out of bed and groped around on the floor for his shoes. Everything was coming back to him clearly now, the poachers, the fire, the lost rhino and her calf, and Chege out there, on the loose, with a gun.

He scrambled into his clothes and a few minutes later was outside. Afra was there already, standing beside Uncle Titus, dragging her fingers through her tangled mop of hair. She turned and shook her head at him even before he'd asked the question.

'No,' she said. 'They haven't caught Chege yet. There's been no sign of him.'

Dr Ibrahim came out through the door after him, carrying his bag of medical supplies.

'Where's Omondi?' he said irritably, peering about him in the gloom.

'He's already in the Land Rover,' Titus told him impatiently. 'Come on, let's go.'

Omandi's big shape was a looming grey shadow in the front seat beside the driver. He turned his head towards Joseph. It was still too dark to be able to see his expression clearly but Joseph could hear the warmth in his voice.

'Good morning, famous poacher catchers,' he said.

He moved up to make room for Titus, who was jumping into the long front seat beside him while Dr Ibrahim heaved himself with difficulty into the back seat beside Joseph and Afra.

The driver started the engine. It roared into life, drowning out the chorus of bird song that had been ringing through the trees.

'Where do we go, *bwana*?' the driver said to Omondi in Swahili.

'To the foot of the Baboon Cliffs,' Omondi answered. 'We'll check first if she went over during the fire.'

'And if we've lost her, then we must find the calf at once,' interrupted Dr Ibrahim. 'There are lions in this park. He won't survive for long.'

'One of the rangers reported that the pride of lions up near the Baboon Cliffs made a good kill yesterday, an old buffalo,' Omondi said, as the driver let in the clutch. 'They may not hunt again until this evening.' He looked up at the rapidly lightening sky. 'If the mother is alive, she'll hide up most of the day among the trees, where the other black rhinos are. They are not like the white rhinos. They are very shy. But she'll probably come down to the lake this morning to drink. We can start there. After that we should go up above the cliffs, where the fire was. Maybe she's still there.'

Dr Ibrahim grunted his consent and the Land Rover set off.

It was still dark but Joseph could see, against the yellow glow of the headlights flooding the road ahead, that Uncle Titus's shoulders were tense and Omondi's hands were gripping the dashboard in front of him.

Every black rhino in the world is precious, he thought. To lose even one – it's a catastrophe.

The trees were gradually thinning now and the Land Rover came out onto the wide open plain that lay along the western edge of Lake Nakuru. The sky was lightening, minute by minute. Then, as suddenly as a flame bursting up from a smouldering log, the edge of the sun's great disc rose above the horizon, and the colours of the earth, the lake and the sky warmed from a faded grey to rich blues and yellows and greens.

The Land Rover was bumping fast along the track that ran across the wide open expanse of grass between the lake on the left and a fringe of trees on the right. Joseph was in the middle of the back seat, flanked by Afra on one side and Dr Ibrahim on the other. His best view was straight ahead, through the windscreen, and he screwed up his eyes, focusing on anything that could possibly be a rhino.

'I think – yes! There! Straight ahead!' he said suddenly, pointing excitedly at a black dot in the distance, that might have been mistaken for a boulder if it hadn't been slowly moving towards the water's edge.

'*Simama!* Stop!' Titus said to the driver.

The Land Rover ground to a halt. Titus and Omondi lifted their powerful binoculars and trained them on the black dot ahead.

'Buffalo,' said Omondi at last, disappointment evident in his voice.

The driver let in the clutch.

'No, wait,' Titus said. 'We'll take a good look round now we've stopped.'

Afra, sitting on Joseph's left, wound down the window of the Land Rover, and the fresh cool air of morning wafted over Joseph's face. The driver had switched the engine off and for a moment there was silence, as everyone scanned the horizon for any sign of a rhino.

Joseph looked down towards the lake. A vast flock of sugar-pink flamingos, hundreds of thousands of them, were feeding in the shallows. They were advancing in one rippling line, their heads bent down in the water, sucking in the rich soup of algae through their curved beaks.

As he watched, something startled them, and they began to rise, their wings flapping in slow motion, their necks stretched out in front, their red legs straight out behind them. They streamed across the pale blue water in a soft rosy cloud.

They looked so beautiful that for a moment Joseph forgot why he was there. He forgot the rhinos, and the desperate search they were engaged in. The Land Rover and the other people in it seemed to melt away and it was as if he was alone, in a vast new-minted world, at the dawn of time, the first man in the Garden of Eden.

Then, between him and the lake, came a strutting line of impala, their twirled horns black above the warm tan of their hides. They raised a flock of little birds who rose from the pale yellow grass in an explosion of feathers, quickly grouping themselves into an aerial formation which turned and wheeled across the lake as if they were obeying some hidden signal.

Another movement caught Joseph's eye. A tawny creature, low on its haunches, was stalking purposefully towards the lake. It stopped for a moment and looked round, and Joseph saw the stern, cat-like face of a lioness. There were terrors in Eden, as well as beauty.

He thought of Chege. He might be lurking somewhere, hiding up in the trees or lying in the long grass, more clever and dangerous than the most powerful lion.

Afra had seen the lioness too. She was twisting her hands together.

'We have to get *on*. We must *find* her!' she muttered.

Titus, in the front seat, had been sweeping the distant landscape intently with his binoculars, but he was focusing now, peering out towards the bottom of the cliff.

'*Twende*,' he said to the driver. 'Over there. Go on.'

The Land Rover roared into life and began to drive fast towards the cliffs. Joseph could feel a new tension among the silent adults. He looked sideways at Dr Ibrahim, but the big man's face was grim and Joseph didn't dare say anything.

Then Afra grabbed his arm.

'Oh no,' she said, her voice sharp with distress. 'Look! Vultures!'

Joseph could see them now. At the foot of the cliff was a shifting mass of birds, moving together like one single pulsating feathery organism, working over a huge, dark, bloodied mass that lay dead on the ground. The birds were fighting each other to get at it, their long naked necks outstretched, tearing off shreds of raw flesh.

'I'm going to throw up,' said Afra, turning her face away. 'I can't look. I can't bear to think of her, just being torn to pieces like this.'

Her voice was breaking.

The Land Rover stopped and Omondi and Titus jumped out. Joseph followed them. He felt a little sick too, but he didn't want anyone to guess it. He forced himself to look. It wasn't easy to make out anything in the flurry of feathers and gore, but Omondi exclaimed with satisfaction, and clapped his hands triumphantly together.

'It's not a rhino!' he called out over his shoulder. 'It's a dead waterbuck!'

Joseph felt a kick of relief in his stomach. He caught Omondi's eye. Anxious sweat had broken out on the man's forehead and Joseph could see that his hands were trembling.

This is terrible for him, he thought. He knows every rhino like a friend. He'll feel it most if . . . if the worst has happened.

Omondi ran back to the Land Rover and climbed onto the bonnet. He stood up and looked through his binoculars for a long moment, raking the rough ground at the bottom of the cliff. Then he jumped down.

'Nothing,' he said to the others. 'The fire was confined only to that area up there.' He pointed up to the top of the cliff where the fringe of green, spilling over the edge, was broken for only a short distance by a section of blackened wood and singed bushes. 'If she went over the cliff it must have been in that small area, but there is nothing here. She's not down here.'

Afra had jumped out of the Land Rover too and now she let out a crow of delight.

'There's hope then!' she said. 'Oh boy, let it be all right. Just let them be safe!'

'Where next?' Titus asked Omondi.

Omondi pointed to the top of the cliff.

'Up there. They were last seen up there.' He stopped and slapped a hand to his forehead. 'Of course! Why didn't I think of it before? She will be where there are ashes. Rhinos like ashes, to lick them. If she is alive, that is where she will be. The other rhinos too, maybe. They will be attracted from their usual place in the woods lower down. Perhaps we'll find all our Nakuru rhinos up there.'

'I hope not,' growled Dr Ibrahim. 'If they're away from their usual ranges, they will be nervous, and nervous rhinos make me very, very nervous.'

It was a bumpy ride up to the top of the cliff and the driver went as fast as he dared. He had to stop once for a huge tortoise, which had obstinately hunkered down in the middle of the road, and twice he braked sharply as nervous water-buck jumped across the track in front of him.

Joseph caught the acrid whiff of burnt vegetation long before they reached the top of the hill. He tapped Omondi tentatively on the arm.

'I don't understand,' he said. 'Why do rhinos lick ashes?'

'Because of the calcium and phosphorus in them,' said Omondi. 'They're minerals that rhinos need. They need salt, too. They used to travel hundreds of miles in the old days, when they were able to move freely round the country, all the way to the Aberdares, where there were salt pans they liked to lick.'

Joseph wrinkled his nose.

'But how do they know they need chemicals like that?' he said.

Omondi turned and smiled at him.

'They crave them,' he said. 'They love the taste. They don't have teachers to give them chemistry lessons in rhino school.'

'They're lucky then,' said Joseph.

They had arrived now at the top of the cliff, and they could see at once the devastation caused by the fire. It had swept swiftly across the ground, catching the dry grass and dead leaves and twigs, and scorching the trunks and tops of the trees.

'We were very fortunate,' Titus said. 'The wind was blowing towards the cliff top. It made the best possible fire break and the fire just burned itself out.'

'That's all very well, Titus,' said Dr Ibrahim, 'but it doesn't answer the real question. Who started the fire? Was it someone who was working with those poachers? If so, then there's a bigger gang than we thought, and our rhinos are still in danger.'

'I think I can tell you,' said Joseph. 'There were tourists here yesterday and they were smoking. If one of them threw a match or a cigarette end out of the car, that would have started a fire.'

'Huh! Tourists! Nothing they do would surprise me,' said Dr Ibrahim impatiently.

'Look! Look!' Omondi had been peering with narrowed eyes through the trees. 'Over there!'

15

RHINO CHARGE!

Everyone craned their necks to look where Omondi was pointing. Joseph had thought that the black shapes under the distant trees were shadows, but his eyes snapped into focus and he saw that they were rhinos. He tried to count them. He could see five, three large ones and two smaller ones. They were moving quietly along, their heads down, snuffling among the ashes that covered the ground in a dusty grey pall.

'There's no calf there,' he said anxiously. 'I can't see him, anyway.'

Omondi had his binoculars trained on the group now. He was studying them carefully.

'The mother's not there, either,' he said, lowering them again.

'How do you know? How can you tell?' said Joseph. 'I can't tell them apart.'

Omondi looked at him with surprise.

'They are all quite different,' he said. 'They are my rhinos. I know them.'

Afra suddenly gave a little scream. She wrenched open the door of the Land Rover and tumbled out.

'Afra! What are you doing? Come back!' Titus called furiously after her.

Afra didn't slacken her pace. Titus snorted with annoyance. He jumped out of the Land Rover, with Joseph right behind him, and was about to race after her when Afra suddenly dived to the ground. She came up again, holding a little animal, which was wriggling furiously in her arms.

She carried it back to Titus, gasping with the effort of keeping hold of it.

'A warthog piglet,' she panted. 'Look. His foot's caught in a drinks can.'

Dr Ibrahim took in the scene at a glance and lumbered down from the Land Rover.

'Put him down on his back,' he said urgently. 'Hold him steady. Joseph, take his head. Be careful, his teeth are sharp. Afra, hold his leg up.'

The little warthog's leg was rammed into the can and the sharp edges of the hole were cutting into his hock, which was beginning to swell. As Dr Ibrahim tried to move it, the piglet squealed, and squirmed more violently than ever.

'Oh please, can't you hurry?' burst out Afra. 'He's in such pain. Look at him!'

Dr Ibrahim shot her a stern look.

'Do you want me to sever his leg? Keep calm. Hold him still. That's right. Titus, bring my bag.'

Titus, frowning with impatience, hurried back to the Land Rover and a second later returned with Dr Ibrahim's medical kit. He set it down and opened it up beside the vet, who had got down on his knees beside the piglet.

Dr Ibrahim took a pair of pliers out of the bag and began deftly to cut back the metal.

'Easy, quiet,' he murmured softly, as the piglet tried to buck himself free. 'Nearly there. Yes – here it comes.'

Gently, he slid the can off the piglet's leg.

'No!' he said sharply to Joseph and Afra, who were relaxing their hold. 'Don't let him go. Wait.'

He picked up a syringe and plunged it into the piglet's round rump.

'What are you giving him?' asked Joseph.

'An antibiotic,' said Dr Ibrahim, getting awkwardly to his feet. 'In case the wound has become infected. All right. You can let him go now.'

Joseph and Afra lifted their hands and the little warthog, with a last indignant squeal, twisted round, scrambled to his feet and ran off on three legs, shaking his long hairy head as if in disbelief.

'It's a good thing his tusks haven't grown yet,' Dr Ibrahim said. 'He would have savaged you. He could have hurt you very badly. Don't ever try to tackle a bigger pig than that.'

Joseph frowned as he watched the piglet run off.

'Who could be so stupid to throw away a can when there are so many animals around?' he said.

'A bunch of low-life idiots,' said Afra, with withering scorn.

Omondi leaned out of the Land Rover window.

'Have you finished with your patient?' he called out. 'Can we go now?'

'Yes, yes.' Dr Ibrahim was brushing ashes from the knees of his bush trousers. 'I'm coming.'

He climbed back into the Land Rover and Titus and Afra jumped in after him. Joseph bent to tie his shoelace, which had come undone. He straightened up, and was face to face with the driver when he saw the man's expression change. He had been looking beyond Joseph, towards the forested path up which the Land Rover had come from the lake below. His eyes were staring and his lips were pulled back from his teeth in a grimace.

'Quick, quick!' he shouted in Swahili. 'Get back in!'

Joseph turned round. Behind him, not more than twenty metres away, was the mother rhino. She had been trotting blindly towards the smell of ashes, but now she had got wind of the Land Rover and the people in it. In one quick glimpse, Joseph took in her rage and pain, the fury of a great and powerful animal who has been pursued and shot at and caught in a fire, and the desperation of a mother who has lost her calf.

Her head was down and she was puffing huge gusts of breath from her nostrils. Her foreleg pawed at the ground.

'Joseph! Get in! Get in!' shouted Titus.

But the rhino had already begun her charge. Instinctively, reacting like an animal himself, Joseph turned and began to run. The world had suddenly been reduced to one need, one desperate aim, to outstrip the huge creature who was bearing down upon him with all the terrifying speed and weight of a train. He didn't have time to look over his shoulder but he knew that she was gaining on him. Desperately, like an antelope running from a lion, he began to twist and turn, but he could hear the great feet swerving nimbly after him, mimicking his every move.

Vaguely, in the distance, he heard the Land Rover's engine roar into life, but all he could focus on was the ground ahead, the trees and scrub beyond the burnt-out field of fire.

The rhino was almost on him now. He could hear the heavy grunting puff of the huge animal's breath. With one last effort, he dived under a bush, and, oblivious to the scratches on his arms and legs, rolled as far under its low branches as he could. The sound of the rhino bursting in after him was the most terrifying thing he had ever heard. He was sure his end had come. He could move no longer. He put up his hands in a futile gesture.

'Please!' he said uselessly. 'Please, go away!'

The rhino's lowered nose was almost in his face. For a moment as long as eternity, she paused, and Joseph actually breathed in her warm breath, and saw the moisture glistening in her leathery grey nostril.

And then, incredibly, she was backing away, tossing her heavy horned head up and down as if satisfied with her victory, trotting off towards the field of ashes.

For a moment, Joseph lay still, too stunned to move. Then everything seemed to happen at once. With a screech of brakes the Land Rover pulled up close by. The door crashed open and Titus shot out. He raced forwards, and pushing through the branches of the bush, sank onto his knees beside Joseph.

'No, no!' he was saying. 'Joseph! My son!'

Joseph struggled to sit up. Titus reached out and gently held him down.

'Wait. Let me check you. Something may be broken.'

Joseph had never seen that look in his stern uncle's face before. Suddenly he wanted to cry.

'I'm all right, Uncle Titus. Really. She didn't hurt me. She stopped just in time.'

'You're sure? Your chest, your head? Nothing happened to them?'

'No.'

Happiness was flooding through Joseph. For the second time in two days he had faced death, but this time he had found something out in the process.

He really loves me, he thought. He called me his son.

Two more faces appeared behind Titus's. Afra's, drawn with shock, and Dr Ibrahim's, lips pursed with anxiety, were peering at them through the bush.

Titus shut his eyes for a long moment, then he called out cheerfully, 'It's all right! She took a good look at him and realized she'd met her match.'

Joseph caught Afra's eye and smiled. She made a little choking sound, then said indignantly, 'Joseph, you gave me such a fright, I thought my heart was going fly right up and out of my throat! I thought you were dead for sure.'

He was crawling out of the bush now, aware for the first time of his scratches.

'Are you glad I'm not?'

She helped him to his feet.

'Oh boy. You go and die on me and I'll never talk to you again.' Her voice changed as curiosity got the better of her. 'What happened? Why did she stop?'

Joseph took a step towards the Land Rover, but for some reason he felt shaky and staggered a little. At once he felt Titus's strong arm round his waist, supporting him and helping him on.

'I don't know,' he said happily. 'She just seemed to change her mind. Maybe she wasn't so angry with me, just with the world in general.'

Back in the Land Rover, he sat between Titus and Afra, trying to control the odd trembling which had broken out all over his body. He felt cold, in spite of the heat of the morning, and Titus's warm, strong, right arm next to him was somehow comforting.

The female rhino, chased away by the Land Rover, had stopped running and was standing in the distance near the edge of the trees, her head drooping, as if the spirit had gone out of her.

'Look at her. She's given up searching for her calf,' said Afra. 'It's just so sad. I can't bear it! Where *is* he? He can't just disappear.'

Then, right on cue, like a little actor running onto a stage, the rhino calf suddenly appeared, trotting confidently across the burnt earth towards his mother. He was calling as he came, a loud mewing sound, that made her jerk up her head and turn towards him.

Friskily, almost bouncing along the ground, her calf ran up to her, and, butting her playfully once or twice with his snub nose, he lunged beneath her belly, looking for her teats.

She waited until he had finished, then turned towards him and sniffed him all over. He ran round her, tossing his small head. Then she wheeled round and slowly, with head held high, she walked away and disappeared among the trees.

The watchers in the Land Rover let out a great

gusting sigh of relief. Joseph, whose heart had lifted again, looked sideways at Omondi, and saw to his surprise that the big man's cheeks were wet.

16

WILDFIRE'S FURY

By the time the Land Rover arrived back at the warden's house, Joseph was himself again.

Titus dropped them off at the place where the short track to the house ran off the road.

'I'll see you later,' he said.

They walked into the kitchen. Nathan was busy, cutting up vegetables for the evening meal.

'Are we too late for breakfast?' said Afra, putting her head on one side in an uncharacteristic attempt to look winsome. 'We're starving.'

Nathan jerked his head in the direction of the living room.

'It is on the table. It is ready for you.'

They went through to where the table had been laid. Freshly cut pawpaws, hard boiled eggs, toast, marmalade and a thermos of tea were waiting for them.

'Why is breakfast so good when you have to wait for it?' said Afra, cramming a huge piece of pawpaw into her mouth. 'This is just the best there is.'

Joseph didn't bother to answer. He was layering butter onto a thick slice of toast.

They finished at last and sat back, replete.

'What now?' said Afra.

'I don't know. We could stay here, perhaps, or play cards, or . . .'

He stopped. He'd run out of ideas.

Afra pushed back her chair and stood up.

'I know. Let's go up to the village and find Two.'

'OK,' said Joseph, following her out of the house.

It was nearly mid-morning already, and the busy scenes of dawn had quietened down. The baboon troop had long since ambled off on their daily quest for food, the Thomson's gazelle had sprinted away on their thin, elegant legs towards the grassy plain near the lake, and even the birds were falling silent.

Afra turned her head and looked back at the road.

'What's that noise?'

'It's only a truck,' said Joseph, as a big vehicle came lumbering down the road towards the main gate.

'From the hotel, probably. It's been delivering supplies,' said Afra, who liked to get things straight in her mind.

They watched the truck idly as it went past. It slowed to take a corner and, as it did so, the canvas cover that hung down loosely over the back swung open.

Afra gasped and grabbed at Joseph's arm.

'Chege! Look, he's hiding in the back!'

Joseph had seen Chege too and was already sprinting after the truck.

'Stop!' he was yelling at the top of his voice. 'Stop!'

'Joseph, are you mad?' shouted Afra, racing after him. 'He's got a gun!'

The truck driver hadn't heard Joseph's shouts above the roar of his engine, but Chege had. He pulled the canvas back and looked out cautiously. The sight of Joseph and Afra seemed to sting him to fury. He had been lying on bales of laundry but now he lurched to his knees, and they saw him grope around on the floor of the truck.

'Joseph, come back!' screamed Afra. 'He's going to shoot!'

Chege had raised the gun to his shoulder. It was pointing at Joseph, but the truck was swaying so erratically on the bumpy road that Chege could not take aim. He seemed to hesitate for a moment, then suddenly threw one leg over the tailboard of the moving truck and vaulted down onto the road, the gun still in his hand.

Joseph and Afra had begun to veer off to the side of the road as soon as they'd seen the gun, but Chege moved so fast that already he was right in front of them, the gun in his hands and murder in his eyes.

They skidded to a halt, turned and began to

race back in the opposite direction. Joseph's brain felt numb. It was too far to run to the warden's house. Chege would have caught them long before they got that far. Instinctively, he made for the nearest cover, the tall square wooden construction of thick planks two metres high. Wildfire's *boma*.

He reached it and dived around the corner with Afra right behind him. They could hear Chege hard on their heels and they raced to the far end of the *boma*. They halted, panting, at the corner. They couldn't hear him now and they didn't know what to do.

The strongly built, narrow entrance corridor, about ten metres long, down which the rhinos had to walk to get out of their big square *boma*, ran out of its far end. Joseph hesitated. Where was Chege? Why hadn't he run round the corner after them? Perhaps he hadn't been so close to them after all. Perhaps he hadn't seen them running round the side of the *boma* and had gone straight on towards the house.

'Where is he? Where did he go?' Afra whispered frantically.

He shook his head at her and put his finger to his lips, then cautiously went to the end of the *boma*'s entrance corridor and peered round it.

He was staring straight into Chege's bloodshot eyes.

With a snarl, Chege leapt forward, then stood,

his finger on the trigger of the gun, pointing it at Joseph.

'I have got you at last,' he said, in a whisper that was more threatening than the loudest shout. 'You have spoiled everything for me. Now I will punish you.'

Joseph and Afra stood frozen to the spot. Joseph couldn't move. He couldn't even think. He heard Afra say, in a calm voice, 'If you shoot us, Nathan will hear. The rangers at the gate will hear. They'll come running. You won't get away.'

Chege's eyes flickered and Joseph could see that he was hesitating, unsure of what to do. He felt his courage return a little, and he was able to think more clearly.

Chege was thinking too. His eyes were raking the wooden wall of the *boma* that rose up behind Joseph and Afra.

'Get up there,' he growled, jerking the gun. 'Onto the crossbar.'

'Listen,' said Joseph. 'Please, Mr Chege . . .'

As soon as he'd said the man's name he realized he'd made a mistake. It seemed to madden Chege still further. His finger tightened on the trigger.

'I said get up there,' he shouted, throwing caution to the winds.

It was as if he didn't care whether he was caught or not. He wanted revenge on Joseph and Afra and nothing else.

Afra had already scrambled up on to the crossbar. The top of the *boma* wall was waist-high to her now.

'I guess we'd better do as he says, Joseph,' she said quietly. 'I reckon he means it.'

Reluctantly, Joseph climbed up beside her. He felt impossibly exposed up here, stuck, unable to run or move. Chege was looking up at them, savouring his moment of power. He was waving the gun towards them, playing with the trigger. Behind him, in the *boma* below, Joseph could hear Wildfire move, snuffling in the dust.

Joseph had broken out into a sweat all over, but he forced his fascinated gaze away from Chege and, looking past him into the distance, pretended to see that someone was coming.

'Here's . . . here comes Uncle Titus!' he said, trying to sound as convincing as he could, though his voice was squeaking with tension.

It was another mistake. Chege, thinking he was running out of time, went mad with fury.

'I'll kill you, I'll kill you!' he shouted, and pulled the trigger.

Nothing happened. The trigger clicked uselessly.

Joseph was trembling violently all over, but with his last reserve of strength he shouted, 'Afra! Jump! Run for it!'

Before they could move, Chege, with a roar like an enraged rhino, ran at the *boma* wall and leapt up onto the crossrail between them. Joseph felt the man's strong hand clamp like a vice on his wrist and sensed that his other arm had closed round Afra's waist.

He's going to throw us into the *boma*! he thought incredulously. We'll be trampled to death by Wildfire!

The great rhino was becoming more active, moving about, his snuffles changing to irritated snorts. Chege's arm, strong as an iron bar, was pushing Joseph backwards, trying to make him topple over into the *boma*. Joseph struggled as hard as he could. He felt the wall of the *boma* tremble as Wildfire began to buffet it with the side of his head.

He felt himself weakening, felt his muscles yielding under the intolerable pressure. Desperately, he fought to loosen Chege's grip, but the man was too strong for him. Then, just as he thought he was about to fall, Chege gave a startled yelp of pain and his fist slackened. Now the big man was leaning back himself, his shoulders over the edge of the *boma*, one hand clasped to his eye. Afra, beside him, was looking astonished at the success of the punch she'd landed in his face, and was poised to inflict another.

Joseph saw his chance, balled his fist and struck. He hit Chege's chin with a sharp clean blow, but nearly missed his footing. Then, as he righted himself, he realized that Chege was toppling over, falling backwards, down into the *boma*.

For a moment he and Afra stood staring at each other in horror. Chege was a thief, a poacher, and a would-be murderer, but they hadn't intended to send him to his death.

They looked down into the *boma*. Chege had fallen awkwardly on his shoulder, but at once he scrambled back onto his feet and, holding his right arm in his left hand, as if he had broken it, he began backing away from the rhino into a corner of the *boma*. Wildfire, alert and disturbed, was sniffing the air, peering round myopically.

Suddenly, his small eyes focused. He had found Chege. He lowered his great head and began to paw the ground with his massive feet, then, with a roar that was almost a scream, and that curdled the blood in Joseph's veins, he charged.

Chege dodged just in time and for a moment it looked as if the rhino would impale himself by his horn in the wall of the *boma*, but at the last moment he wheeled, skidding in the dust, and then he was pounding after Chege again.

'We have to help him!' gasped Afra. 'We have to pull him out!'

'How can we?' said Joseph. 'He'd pull us down with him.'

He was running his eyes round the *boma* looking for a solution. They rested on the door that gave onto the tunnel-like entrance. It was a thick wooden panel that had been dropped down into place between two grooved posts.

'Help me get the door open!' he called to Afra, beginning to work his way along the crossrail towards the entrance.

She followed his glance, understood his idea, and without a word jumped down from the crossrail and began to race round the *boma* to the far side of the entrance so that they would be able to work together on lifting the door from both sides.

Chege was distraught and his breath was coming in gasping moans. He was tiring rapidly, though he was still managing, just, to dodge out of the range of the rhino's plunging horn.

Joseph wasted no time in looking at him. He was at the door now, trying to lift it from above. It was a solid piece of wood and brutally heavy.

'Afra, where are you? Come on, help me!' he muttered through gritted teeth, straining on the rope that lifted the door.

He heard a heavy, metallic clang at the other end of the entrance corridor and a moment later Afra was in front of him, up on the crossrail at the far side of the door.

'Pull! Pull!' shouted Joseph.

He could feel her contribution now. The door began to move. It was as if it had been stuck, because now, with two of them working on it, it rose easily in its grooves.

Joseph looked back and down into the *boma*. Wildfire had cornered Chege, who was cowering against the far wall, his eyes wild and staring. The rhino seemed to be gathering himself for one final assault.

'Chege! The door! It's open!' screamed Afra.

Chege looked, and Joseph saw hope and astonishment chase each other over his face. Then he moved, quick as a snake, darting sideways, and hared across the open space of the *boma* before Wildfire had turned.

With a grunt of pain as his broken arm hit the door post, Chege was through, out of the *boma* and inside the long entrance tunnel.

'Drop the door! Quick!' shouted Joseph.

Wildfire was pounding across the *boma* now in pursuit. For one dreadful moment, Joseph felt the door stick, then, as he and Afra released the ropes together, it crashed down, right in front of Wildfire's nose.

The huge rhino juddered to a halt, then wheeled round and began to trot round his *boma*, snorting angrily, hunting for his prey.

A terrible thought occurred to Joseph.

'Afra, the end of the tunnel!' he said. 'It's open! Chege will get out!'

Afra grinned at him.

'No he won't,' she said. 'I shut it when I was

running round to help you. We've got him. We've caught him – as snug as a bug!'

Later, much later, when the harsh colours of midday were already deepening into the softer glow of late afternoon, Joseph, Afra and Titus were leaning over the side of the *boma* once again. Chege had long since been hauled out of the entrance tunnel by a furious Omondi and a pair of rangers, and had been taken off in handcuffs to join the others in the police station.

Joseph looked down wonderingly at the great creature. He was calm again now, sleepy almost, and was nibbling delicately at the leaves of a grey-green bush that Omondi had thrown down to him.

'Why's he shaking his head like that?' said Afra.

'That plant tastes bitter,' replied Titus.

'He likes it though,' said Joseph. 'Look at him.'

Joseph felt confused and churned up inside. He had never imagined he could live through so much in the space of only forty-eight hours.

'What will happen to Chege and those other two, Uncle Titus?' he said.

'Prison,' Titus said grimly. 'It's what they deserve. The two outsiders were only a couple of stupid loafers from Nairobi. They could never have done something like that on their own. But Chege – he was in a position of trust. The Kenya Wildlife Service trusted him, and he betrayed us and the animals. He should stay in prison for a long time.'

He stopped talking and they all fell silent, watching Wildfire, who had finished eating and was absentmindedly scratching the back of his left hock with the side of his right foot.

'He's so calm now,' said Afra. 'It's like he's got something out of his system. He's not even so nervous of us being here and talking.'

'Oh, there's plenty of fire left in him,' said Titus. 'Don't be fooled. If you got too close to him, you would very soon discover it.'

Afra shuddered.

'As if I would!'

Titus looked down at Joseph. 'You're very quiet. Have you swallowed your tongue?'

Joseph shook his head. He wanted to explain to his uncle what he'd been feeling – how he'd thought several times over the last two days that he was about to die, how he'd been weak and trembling one moment, then brave and confident the next, and how he'd started thinking about his father. He wanted to tell Titus how he'd felt warm and strengthened up there on the cliff when Titus had called him his son.

Instead he said, 'I'll never pass my science exam. It will never make any sense to me.'

Titus burst out laughing, making Wildfire skitter nervously. The three of them jumped down from the wall of the *boma* so as to leave him in peace, and began to walk back to the house.

'Joseph,' Titus said at last, 'you have learnt more science in the last two days then you have probably ever learned in your life. What was Dr Ibrahim telling you about getting the balance of chemicals right in the tranquillizer darts? And what was Omondi saying about the rhino's need for phosphorus and calcium and salts? That's chemistry, isn't it?'

'Is it?' said Joseph. 'But it's interesting!'

He frowned, thinking things out. Science would be all right if it was something he could understand, something to do with real things, like rhinos. He'd really like it, too, if he could see how it could be useful, for things like solar panels. It might even be fun then.

'Hello,' said a cheerful voice behind them.

They all turned round.

'Two!' Joseph and Afra said together. 'Are you all right?'

Two puffed out his chest.

'I am very well. Poachers, rhinos, knocks on the head – I am so tough I can take them all!' He stopped, grinned and rubbed his head. 'Eh, but I heard how you caught Chege. That was very clever! Very wonderful!'

Titus was looking puzzled.

'How did you get into the park again? There

aren't any more holes in the fence that we didn't know about, are there?'

'No, sir.' Two's cheeky manner dropped away as he answered Titus. 'The rangers have already mended the secret entrance. But the fellows on the gate, they heard about me. Aha, they said, you are the champion wonder boy who catches poachers.' His chest was swelling again. 'So they let me come in. Me and my friends.'

As if waiting for a signal, three other boys came forward.

'This is Eliezer,' said Two, dragging one of them forward. 'He knows about cars.'

'So I believe.' Titus shook Eliezer's hand respectfully. 'A bit too much about cars. Perhaps we can find you a job when you're older, looking after the KWS vehicles. Otherwise you might be tempted to use your talents in a life of crime.'

Eliezer looked shocked.

'Crime? No, no, I do not like crime and criminals.'

Titus punched him lightly on the shoulder and turned to the other two boys.

'I'm only teasing. Now, who are you two?'

'They are Daniel and Caleb,' said Two. 'The ones in the car. They jumped up from behind and caught the poacher.'

'You really are champions.' Titus's voice was full of admiration. 'What are you going to do when you leave school? Join the police force? Become commandos? Do stunts on TV?'

Daniel shook his head.

'We are going to be footballers,' he said.

'We're going to play in the Kenyan national team and win the World Cup,' said Caleb seriously. 'So we have come to ask Joseph if he will come and play with us. And you, sir, if you like.'

'Oh?' Afra was scowling at them. 'So it's the same old story, is it? Joseph and Uncle Titus can play, but I can't.'

The three boys looked confused.

'We are not used to playing with girls,' said Eliezer. 'In our village girls don't play football.'

'Well I do,' said Afra, 'and I'm good.'

'It's true,' nodded Joseph. 'She's good.'

Two grinned at her.

'OK,' he said. 'You can make a guest appearance.'

'It will have to be a farewell appearance too,' said Titus. 'We're leaving in the morning.'

Two's face fell.

'You are going? Already?'

'I have to get back to Nairobi,' said Titus. 'I have a lot of work waiting for me there.'

Joseph felt, to his surprise, a sudden, almost pleasant feeling of anticipation.

'So have I,' he said.

17
KIMEU'S GIFT

Joseph walked up the short driveway to Professor Tovey's old house, under the arching canopy of trees. The bag of books on his back was heavy and he was looking forward to putting it down.

He went round to the kitchen where Sarah, his mother, Professor Tovey's housekeeper, was ironing Afra's school uniform. She looked up at him anxiously.

'How was it today?'

'Good, Mama.' Joseph put his bag down with relief and twisted his head round to inspect the shoulders of his shirt in case dye from the straps had stained them. He was so proud of his new school uniform that he couldn't bear to think of the slightest blemish spoiling it.

'You understand your teachers? Your marks are good?'

'Mama, I don't have any marks yet. The term only started three days ago.'

Joseph smiled at her. Since he'd retaken his exam two months ago, and won his scholarship to the new school, an unexpected confidence had uplifted him. He would do well, he knew that for

sure. He'd work, and study, and learn everything
he could. And he'd enjoy it.

Sarah put the iron down and went across to
the shelf by the window where she kept her torch
and the collection of postcards that Afra had sent
her over the years.

'There is a letter for you. I don't know the
writing.'

She turned it over in her hands, looked up at
Joseph curiously and handed it to him. Then she
burst out laughing.

'Receiving letters! Like a man!'

Joseph tore open the envelope. It was from
Two.

Dear Friend,

*I am well and I send you most friendly
greetings from Eliezer and Caleb and Daniel.*

*I write to tell you news of our big friend
with the horn. He has left his boma now. He
ate many good plants there and knows them.
He is healthy. He had two big fights with the
other bull rhinos. I did not see the fights
because our secret way to go into the park
has been closed down, but the rangers, they
told me. Wildfire was very good at the
fighting and he was not hurt. The other rhinos
were not hurt too much too. Now Wildfire
has made his own range for himself and he is*

OK. Last week, Omondi saw him with the female, our one, whom we saved.

Dear Friend, do not forget your friend, Two-brains. I am very happy if I can hear from you. You and Afra are my good mates. The other boys call me Two now. It is a good name. I like it.

Come and see us again in Nakuru. We are waiting for you!!!

God bless.

Two

Sarah had gone out of the kitchen, taking the washing basket under her arm to fetch in the washing that was drying outside on the line. Joseph stood and stared out of the window. He hardly saw the huge cage where Stumpy, Afra's goose, spent the night, or the scarlet red hibiscus bush, or the corner of his mother's vegetable patch. He was back in Nakuru, lying under a bush, putting up his hands, his sole protection, against the juggernaut of bone and horn and hide that was furiously seeking him out.

Why, at the very moment when he was at the rhino's mercy, had she backed away? Was it because she had seen how helpless Joseph was, a threat she need no longer fear? Was it because she had heard the Land Rover bearing down on her from behind, and it had scared her away? Or was it because her anger hadn't really been directed towards Joseph at all? Perhaps it had been a general rage, a kind of welling up of aggression and hostility, mixed with anxiety about her calf, and distrust, and a fear of humans.

He smiled at himself. What was the good of trying to work out a rhino's feelings? She was a rhino. He was a human. How could he know what she felt? She lived in a different, parallel, mysterious world.

He heard steps outside and Afra came into the kitchen. She flung her school bag carelessly down on the floor.

'Where's Sarah? I'm hungry.'

'She's bringing in the washing.'

'Oh? Is she outside?' Afra opened the fridge and poured herself a glass of milk. 'Perhaps the old man found her then.'

'What old man?'

'I don't know. There was an old guy by the gate. Wrapped in a blanket. He looked as if he came from up country.'

Joseph's brows twitched together. He craned his neck out of the window. Sarah stood by the washing line, the half-filled basket at her feet. In front of her, tall, stately and still, stood his grandfather.

Joseph ran out of the kitchen.

'Grandfather!' he shouted joyously.

Kimeu turned towards him. His face lit up with a smile.

Joseph felt suddenly shy. It was strange seeing Grandfather here, in Nairobi. He seemed older and smaller, as if the city had diminished him. He looked oddly fragile, too. Joseph felt an unfamiliar urge to look after him. The feeling disturbed him. He'd always gone to Grandfather for protection before. It was as if the tables had been turned.

'Are you well? Is Mwende well?' he asked, not knowing what else to say.

'She's well.' Kimeu's voice was deep and the sound of it gave Joseph a rush of love for him.

'You're tired,' he said. 'Come inside and take some rest.'

He tried to take Kimeu's arm.

'No, wait.' The old man pushed his hand away. 'First I have something to give you.'

He walked stiffly over to the gate, then looked round, surprised. Something had been eating the blue flowers of the plumbago plant that sprawled lavishly over the Toveys' front fence, but whatever it had been, it was not there now.

Then Joseph heard a scream from the house and a burst of laughter. Afra came running out through the front door.

'Joseph!' she called out. 'Guess what? There's a goat in the house. He's the darlingest little thing, with curly brown hair, and he's been eating the papers in Prof's study!'

A slow smile spread over Joseph's face and he turned to Kimeu.

'My goat,' he said.

Kimeu nodded.

'Your goat. A gift for a boy when he becomes a man.'

Elizabeth Laird
Wild Things 2:
BABOON ROCK

Deep in the African bush! It'll be the best birthday of Afra's life.

Her present is a trip to Baboon Rock, living in the wild among elephants, cheetahs and zebra. Tom and Joseph are sharing the adventure and, best of all, her busy father is coming too.

But her dad breaks his promise. And Afra's disappointment makes her disobey all the rules. After dark, she creeps out alone, desperate to save a baby baboon. And herself becomes the prey of some hungry night hunters . . .

WILD THINGS titles
available from Macmillan

The prices shown below are correct at the time of going to press. However, Macmillan Publishers reserve the right to show new retail prices on covers which may differ from those previously advertised.

ELIZABETH LAIRD

1. Leopard Trail	0 330 37148 7	£2.99
2. Baboon Rock	0 330 37149 5	£2.99
3. Elephant Thunder	0 330 37150 9	£2.99
4. Rhino Fire	0 330 37151 7	£2.99
5. Red Wolf	0 330 37152 5	£2.99

All Macmillan titles can be ordered at your local bookshop or are available by post from:

Book Service by Post
PO Box 29, Douglas, Isle of Man IM99 1BQ

Credit cards accepted. For details:
Telephone: 01624 675137
Fax: 01624 670923
E-mail: bookshop@enterprise.net

Free postage and packing in the UK.
Overseas customers: add £1 per book (paperback)
and £3 per book (hardback).